THE INVITATION

W. CAWTHON

DEDICATION

Dedication
This book is dedicated to anyone carrying grief that feels too heavy to name.

To those who have lost someone they loved and wake each day feeling that absence echo through everything.

To those living with depression, whose minds wage quiet wars no one else can see.

To those who have faced suicidal thoughts and stayed—even when staying felt impossible.

To those marked by trauma, whether recent or long past, whose lives were divided into *before* and *after*.

We are with you! This is for you.

For the nights when sleep would not come.

For the days when breathing felt like work.

For the moments when you questioned your worth, your strength, or your place in the world.

May we remind you that you are not alone in your pain.

That what you feel is real, valid, and deserving of compassion.

That surviving does not mean you are weak—it means you are still fighting.

If you are grieving, may you find gentleness with yourself.

If you are hurting, may you find understanding instead of judgment.

If you are lost, may you find even the smallest light to guide you forward.

You are worthy of love, of help, and of healing.

Your story does not end in the chapter you are living now.

This book is written for the ones that lost the battle and the ones that are still fighting with hope that you keep going—

one breath, one page, one moment at a time.

CONTENTS

CHAPTER ONE

CHAPTER ONE

THE PLACE WITHOUT MERCY

B efore Caligo had a name, it was a condition.

It was born in a place that was not hell, though many would have called it that. Hell, at least, promised judgment and conclusion. This place had neither. It was a fold in existence where suffering did not end—it *echoed*. Pain there was not inflicted; it was *remembered*. Every regret, every moment of helplessness, every scream that never found an ear pooled together like stagnant water. Time did not move forward. It sank.

Caligo emerged from that stagnation.

At first it had no shape, only hunger. Not hunger for flesh or blood—those were crude appetites. Caligo hungered for **repetition**. It fed on the way a mind replays trauma, on the way memory sharpens pain instead of dulling it. The place taught it that the cruelest torment was not violence, but *recall*. The endless return to a moment you would give anything to escape.

It learned by listening.

Caligo learned that mortals break not when pain is greatest, but when pain becomes *familiar*. When the mind stops fighting and begins expecting the blow. When hope rots into ritual despair.

That was when Caligo learned how to leave.

It found cracks—thin seams where grief wore reality down. Hospital rooms after the machines went quiet. Wreckage sites where bodies were already gone but screams remained. Bedrooms where children stared at ceilings long after the shouting stopped downstairs. Caligo slipped through those moments, clothed in the residue of what had already happened.

It did not arrive with thunder or flame.

It arrived with memory.

At first, its victims thought they were dreaming. A moment replayed itself with uncanny clarity: the smell of antiseptic, the metallic taste of fear, the sound of a voice begging—or worse, silent. Then it happened again. Exactly the same. No variation. No mercy. The mind rebelled, tried to change the outcome, tried to scream—but memory does not allow intervention.

Caligo watched.

It learned patience from trauma itself. It did not rush. It let the repetition grind its victims down until time lost meaning. Until they stopped distinguishing past from present. Until pain was no longer something that happened—but something that *was*.

Only then did Caligo speak.

Not aloud. Not in words. It spoke as an *offer*.

Let me in.

The first time Caligo was invited inside a human mind, it learned something new.

Relief.

The pain stopped. The memory went quiet. The victim felt peace so sudden it felt holy. They mistook the silence for salvation.

Then Caligo took control.

It did not kill out of anger. It killed out of **completion**. The body was simply the final memory to create—the one that would echo longest in the place it came from. The death was never quick. It was symbolic, intimate, tailored to the original trauma. Caligo learned that the most horrifying endings were the ones that felt *inevitable*, like the last line of a story already read a thousand times.

When the body was finished, Caligo left.

It carried the echo with it.

That echo made it stronger.

And so Caligo returned to the cracks, more defined now, more deliberate. No longer a condition.

Now a being.

Now a name waiting to be remembered.

CHAPTER TWO

THE SHAPE OF CALIGO

C aligo does not look the same to everyone.

It wears what the mind can endure just long enough to surrender.

Most often, it appears as a silhouette—too dark for darkness, as though light itself avoids it. Its edges ripple, never quite still, like smoke remembering it was once solid. Looking directly at Caligo is difficult; the eyes slide away as if the brain refuses to complete the image.

But when Caligo chooses to be seen, it is unforgettable.

Its body is tall and elongated, proportions subtly wrong, like a human stretched by grief instead of gravity. Its surface resembles charred skin and wet shadow at once, cracked in places where pale, flickering images move beneath—*memories*. Not Caligo's memories, but stolen ones. Faces screaming silently. Hands reaching. Mouths open in unfinished sentences.

Its face—if it can be called that—is smooth where features should be. No eyes. No mouth. Yet victims swear they feel its gaze drilling into the most fragile part of them, like fingers pressing on a bruise.

When Caligo speaks, the sound does not travel through air. It blooms inside the skull, using the victim's own voice, fractured and layered. Every sentence overlaps with the echo of the traumatic memory currently looping, so that the past and the present bleed together.

You're tired, it says.

You've already survived this.

You don't have to anymore.

Caligo does not threaten. It does not command. It **waits**.

It understands that invitation is the purest form of surrender. Consent is the lock that keeps it out—and the key that lets it in.

Once inside, Caligo inhabits the mind like a guest who rearranges the furniture while smiling politely. Thoughts become sluggish. Pain dulls. Fear softens. The victim feels whole for the first time since the trauma began.

That is when Caligo shows them the final memory.

Not a replay—but a rehearsal.

It guides the body with unnatural tenderness, making every movement deliberate, ceremonial. The world narrows. Sounds stretch. Sensations become vivid in a way that feels wrong, heightened beyond what flesh should perceive. There is no panic anymore—only clarity. The victim understands, with awful certainty, that this moment will be remembered forever.

And that is the point.

Caligo leaves the body at the instant the memory becomes permanent. It slips free as life drains away, carrying the echo back to the place without mercy. The echo screams there endlessly, enriching the stagnant sea of suffering from which Caligo was born.

That is how Caligo survives.

That is how it grows.

It is not a demon of death.

It is a demon of **ending pain by preserving it**.

And somewhere, right now, a memory is repeating itself for the hundredth time.

Caligo is listening.

CHAPTER THREE

CHAPTER THREE

THE FIRST INVITATION

The pain always returned at night.

Evan learned that early on, before the whispering began—before the air thickened and the walls felt closer than they should. During the day, the memory dulled. It hid behind routine. Coffee. Emails. The illusion of control. But at night, when the world dimmed and distractions retreated, it came back with teeth.

The accident.

The first scream came at 2:17 a.m.

Evan jerked awake on his couch, heart battering his ribs, fingers clawing at fabric that wasn't there. For a moment he didn't know where he was—only that something had gone wrong, catastrophically wrong, and that he was late.

Late.

That word followed him everywhere now.

The apartment was dark except for the microwave clock glowing an accusing green. 2:17. The same time. It was always the same time.

He pressed the heels of his palms into his eyes, breathing through his teeth the way he'd taught patients to do through pain. The smell was back already—sterile alcohol wipes and latex gloves layered over something sweeter. Childish. Shampoo. The kind with cartoon animals on the bottle.

"No," he whispered to the empty room, but his mind didn't listen. He was back in the pediatric ward.

The lights were too bright, buzzing faintly, the way they always did during night rounds when the hospital felt hollowed out and fragile. Evan saw himself at the medication cart, name badge crooked, exhaustion clinging to him like a second skin. Twelve-hour shift turning into sixteen because someone had called out. He remembered the weight behind his eyes, the quiet confidence of routine. He had done this a thousand times.

He had not checked the dosage twice.

In the apartment, Evan slid off the couch and sank to the floor, back against the coffee table. His hands trembled as if they belonged to someone else. In his head, he watched his own hands draw the medication into the syringe. Clear liquid. Clean. Correct—until it wasn't.

He remembered the child's room. The low beeping of the monitor. Stickers on the wall. A stuffed dinosaur slumped against a pillow, one glass eye missing. The boy's name pulsed behind Evan's eyes like a bruise. He never said it out loud anymore. Saying it felt like opening a door.

In the memory, the child smiled at him. Trusted him.

That was the part that never changed.

Evan's stomach twisted. He dug his fingernails into his forearms until he felt skin break, welcomed the sting. Punishment, his mind whispered. Deserved.

He remembered pushing the medication, slow and careful, narrating like he always did. Remembered the moment the monitor's rhythm faltered—not enough to alarm, just enough. A hitch. A stutter. He had frowned, leaned closer, told himself it was nothing.

In the present, Evan rocked back and forth, breath coming shallow. "You fixed it," he told himself, voice cracking. "You did everything right after."

That was true, in a way. He had acted fast when the child seized. Called the code. Followed protocol with shaking hands and a smile that didn't belong on his face. He had watched doctors flood the room, had stepped back into the blur of bodies and commands.

He had watched the monitor go flat.

The hospital investigation had been brief. Charts reviewed. Timelines adjusted. Another nurse's initials appeared where his should have been. A decimal point drifted into the right place. No one asked the questions that mattered. Evan hadn't offered answers.

He had gone home that morning and vomited until his throat bled.

Now the nightmare shifted, as it always did. The scene replayed, but slower, crueler. This time Evan noticed details he'd missed before: the way the child's fingers twitched, reaching. The sound the mother made when she arrived—a sound that wasn't a scream yet, but would be. The way the dinosaur fell to the floor when someone brushed past it.

In the apartment, Evan slammed his fist into the wall. The pain was sharp and grounding. White bloomed behind his eyes.

"I'm sorry," he whispered, over and over, to the peeling paint, to the memory, to no one.

Sleep deprivation had begun to blur the edges of things. Sometimes, during waking hours, he swore he heard the monitor beeping in the distance. Sometimes he smelled shampoo in the grocery store and had to abandon his cart. Once, at work, he'd caught his reflection in a supply room mirror and for a split second saw a child standing behind him, face pale, eyes accusing.

He had laughed then. A brittle sound that made his coworkers stare.

Now, still half-trapped in the nightmare, Evan saw himself standing at the foot of the hospital bed again. Only this time, the child sat up.

The boy's eyes were open, too open, glassy and wrong. His mouth moved, but no sound came out. The monitor began to scream.

Evan's chest seized. He pressed his forehead to his knees, gasping. "I know," he sobbed. "I know what I did."

The child tilted his head, mirroring the way he had when he was alive. Confused. Hurt. Trusting, still. That was the worst part. Not anger. Not hatred.

Trust.

"You didn't check," the child said at last, voice soft and echoing, layered with the alarm's shriek.

Evan screamed and the apartment swallowed it.

When the nightmare finally released him, dawn was leaking through the blinds in thin gray lines. His throat was raw. His body ached like he'd been beaten. He lay curled on the floor, staring at nothing, mind still looping.

He thought of confession, sometimes. Of turning himself in, of letting the truth destroy what was left of his life. But another part of him—the part that had nudged that decimal point—whispered that suffering was enough. That living like this was a sentence worse than prison.

He pushed himself upright, wiping his face with shaking hands. In a few hours, he would go back to the hospital. Back to the beeping machines. Back to the trust in patients' eyes.

As he stood, a faint sound drifted through the apartment.

A monitor's steady beep.

Evan froze.

The sound continued, slow and patient, as if waiting for him to make another mistake.

He tried not to think of it. Tried not to remember the sound—the wet crunch, the sudden absence of weight, the way silence screamed louder than the impact. But memory was not something he *visited*. It was something that lived inside him, patient and waiting.

Tonight, it was worse.

He lay on his side, facing the wall, counting breaths. In for four. Hold. Out for six. The therapist had said grounding techniques worked best when practiced consistently. Evan practiced until his lungs burned.

Then the room changed.

It was subtle at first. The hum of the refrigerator downstairs deepened, stretching into a low vibration that settled in his bones. The shadows along the baseboard lengthened, bending toward him like fingers testing the air.

"No," he whispered, though he didn't know to whom.

The smell came next.

The weird metallic smell of Blood.

The mattress dipped behind him.

His heart stuttered violently, slamming against his ribs as if trying to escape. He didn't turn around. He couldn't. The air pressed down on his chest, thick and suffocating.

Again, his mind screamed. *Not again.*

The accident replayed without mercy.

The scream that wasn't loud enough. The child's face—confused, then gone. Over and over, the moment reset like a broken recording. Every detail sharpened, refined, perfected into torment.

Evan clawed at the sheets.

"I can't," he sobbed. "Please. I can't do this again."

That was when it spoke.

Not aloud—not in sound—but directly *inside* him, sliding between thoughts like a blade through muscle.

You already are.

The presence leaned closer. He felt it then—not touch, but *occupation*. A pressure behind his eyes. A cold intimacy.

Reliving is survival, it murmured. *Pain is memory. Memory is punishment.*

Tears streamed into his hairline. "What do you want?"

The thing did not answer immediately. It allowed the memory to play once more—slower this time, stretching the agony, forcing Evan to feel every second he'd begged time to erase.

Then, gently:

I want to help you stop.

The room went utterly still.

Evan swallowed hard. "How?"

A pause. A deliberate one.

Invite me in.

The words felt wrong—like splinters in his mind. He shook his head violently. "No. No, you're lying."

Am I? it asked, almost kindly. *How many nights have you begged for silence? For sleep? For forgiveness you will never grant yourself?*

The memory surged again, harsher now. Louder. The child's scream echoed endlessly, overlapping itself until Evan couldn't tell where one replay ended and the next began.

He screamed.

"Stop! Please—just stop!"

The presence wrapped around his panic like a lover.

Say it, it coaxed. *Let me inside. I will make it quiet.*

His resistance crumbled under exhaustion, guilt, and the unbearable promise of peace.

"I... I invite you," Evan whispered.

The demon entered him like a breath he didn't remember taking.

The pain vanished.

Instantly.

Evan collapsed into sleep with a sigh of relief, unaware of the smile stretching his face into something no longer human.

Downstairs, the knife block rattled softly.

CHAPTER FOUR

CHAPTER FOUR

WHAT REMAINS AFTER SILENCE

E van woke smiling.

That alone should have terrified him.

Sunlight spilled across the bedroom, warm and forgiving. No headache. No nausea. No memory clawing at the back of his mind. The accident—*the accident*—was distant, muted, like something he'd read about long ago.

For the first time in years, his thoughts were quiet.

"Thank you," he whispered to the empty room.

The response came instantly.

You're welcome.

The voice was clearer now. Settled. Comfortable.

He stood and moved through the house as if floating, every step purposeful yet detached. When he passed the hallway mirror, he paused.

His reflection looked... wrong.

His eyes were brighter. Too focused. And when he smiled again, it lingered a fraction too long.

You feel lighter, the demon observed. *Unburdened.*

"I do," Evan said. "I feel—normal."

You feel empty, it corrected gently.

He didn't argue.

The day passed in a blur. Evan called in sick. He ignored messages. The world felt irrelevant, distant, as though he were already stepping away from it.

By afternoon, the demon began to guide him.

There is something you must do.

Evan felt the pull then—subtle but insistent. A tightening behind his sternum. A direction.

"What?" he asked.

Finish your penance.

He found himself in the kitchen without remembering the walk there. The knives gleamed under fluorescent light, pristine and expectant.

His hands trembled—not with fear, but anticipation.

A flicker of resistance sparked deep within him. "This isn't what we agreed to."

The demon's presence expanded, filling every corner of his mind.

You invited me in to stop the pain, it reminded him. *And I have. This is merely the final step.*

Memory stirred—not of the accident, but of something else. A shadowed awareness. A sense of wrongness.

"People will find me," Evan whispered.

They always do.

The demon leaned closer, its voice now layered—many voices overlapping, each one once human.

And they will wonder. And they will hurt. And when the pain becomes unbearable...

Understanding bloomed too late.

"You'll move on," Evan said hoarsely.

I always do.

His hand closed around the knife.

The handle was colder than he expected, biting into his palm as if it recognized him. His fingers tightened automatically, tendons standing out beneath his skin. For a brief, treacherous moment, he wondered how many meals it had prepared—how many ordinary days it had served without complaint.

The demon guided his wrist upward.

Steady, it whispered, its voice now threaded through his muscles, his breath, the pulse hammering at his throat. *Don't rush. This is an offering.*

Evan staggered backward until his spine struck the counter. The impact knocked the air from his lungs in a wet gasp. His knees buckled, but the thing inside him held him upright, locking his joints with unnatural strength.

"No," he croaked—not as a plea, but as a reflex, the last syllable of a language he no longer spoke.

The knife pressed against his abdomen.

The first cut was shallow.

A testing wound.

Skin parted with a soft, obscene sound. Pain flared white-hot, sudden and blinding, and Evan screamed—loud enough that his throat tore, loud enough that his voice fractured into something animal.

The demon did not let him pull away.

There it is, it murmured approvingly. *You remember how to suffer.* The blade slid deeper.

Evan felt layers give way—resistance, then warmth, then something *slick* that made the knife slip sideways. Blood poured over his hands, dark and impossibly hot, pooling at his feet in spreading petals. His legs trembled violently, muscles spasming as shock tried to steal him away.

The demon denied him that mercy.

Look, it commanded.

Evan's gaze dropped unwillingly to the ruin opening in his stomach. He saw glistening tissue, pale loops pressing forward as if curious, as if trying to escape before the rest of him failed. The smell hit him next—iron and rot and something sweet that turned his stomach even as it spilled outward.

He gagged, choking on his own breath.

"Please," he sobbed, tears streaking blindly down his face. "You said it would stop."

It has, the demon replied calmly. *This pain is different. This pain ends.*

The knife was drawn upward now, slow and deliberate, sawing through muscle. Evan felt himself tearing open, felt heat rush out of him as if his body were emptying itself onto the tile. His screams dissolved into wet gargles as blood filled his mouth, dribbling down his chin in thick ropes.

His knees finally gave out.

He collapsed hard, back striking the floor, organs shifting horribly inside him. The demon forced his grip tighter, angling the blade toward his throat.

Almost, it crooned. *Hold still.*

The final cut was clean.

The world narrowed to pressure, then release. A red warmth soaked his collarbone, his neck, his hair. His heartbeat thundered once—twice—then stuttered, confused by the sudden emptiness.

As Evan's vision dimmed, the demon leaned fully into him, savoring the moment of departure.

Thank you for the shelter, it whispered. *You were very easy to live in.*

Evan died with his mouth open, eyes glassy and fixed on nothing.

Minutes later, his body went slack.

The demon slipped free.

Chapter Five

CHAPTER FIVE
THE WOMAN WHO COULDN'T LEAVE

The memory began with a red light.

It always did.

Emma stood at the crosswalk with her hands locked around a paper cup that had long since gone cold. The street smelled of rain and exhaust. The sound of traffic layered itself into something almost musical—engines rising, brakes sighing, horns punctuating the air like irritated birds. She knew this moment. Knew it the way one knows their own pulse.

She had been here before.

Again.

And again.

And again.

The light stayed red.

A child laughed somewhere behind her. A delivery truck idled to her left. Her reflection stared back at her from the glass of a bus shelter—eyes hollow, shoulders tense, mouth set as if bracing for impact. She wanted to turn around. She always wanted to turn around.

She never could.

The scream came next.

Not from the street.

From inside her skull.

Her daughter's scream—sharp, panicked, unfinished. The sound dragged Emma backward through time, tearing the present apart like wet paper. The street dissolved. The crosswalk vanished.

Now there was a hospital hallway. Machines beeped in a rhythm that felt cruelly cheerful. A doctor was speaking, but his words blurred into noise because Emma already knew what he was going to say.

She had lived this moment more times than she could count.

The worst sound was tires screaming against asphalt, a sound that tore through the air like fabric ripping under too much strain. It lived in her now, lodged somewhere behind her eyes, replaying whenever her thoughts slowed just enough to catch it.

The hospital room was too white. Too clean. It smelled like disinfectant and grief, though the second scent wasn't real—Emma knew that. She sat rigid in the plastic chair beside the bed, hands folded so tightly her fingers had gone numb. The small body beneath the sheet did not move. It looked smaller than it should have, as if the world had already begun erasing her daughter.

Emma's gaze fixed on the faint outline of her child's face beneath the thin hospital blanket. Pale. Still. Peaceful in a way that felt obscene.

The doctor had spoken gently. Everyone had spoken gently. Phrases like *severe trauma* and *we did everything we could* drifted through her memory like smoke, impossible to grab hold of. None of it mattered. None of it changed the image burned into her mind.

Her phone vibrating in her coat pocket.

Her irritation.

The way she'd turned her head for just a second.

She squeezed her eyes shut, but the memory surged forward anyway.

They had been walking home from the park. Emma remembered the way the sun hung low and golden, the way her daughter skipped along the sidewalk, humming a tuneless song. Emma had been tired—always tired—her patience thin from bills and work and the constant, grinding noise of adulthood. When her phone buzzed, she'd sighed, already annoyed at whoever needed her now.

"Stay right here," she had said absently, fingers already swiping the screen.

The memory twisted then, sharpening like broken glass.

She had not waited for an answer.

A laugh—high and bright—cut through the air. The slap of sneakers on concrete. Emma looked up just in time to see her daughter dart forward, a blur of color and movement, chasing something invisible. A butterfly. A leaf. Nothing at all.

"Sweetie—"

The word barely left her mouth before the sound came.

Screaming tires.

Impact.

The world seemed to lurch, folding in on itself as her daughter's body was thrown aside like something discarded. Emma remembered the way her phone hit the ground, the screen spiderwebbing, as if it, too, understood something had broken beyond repair.

Back in the hospital room, Emma opened her eyes.

The monitor beside the bed was quiet now. No beeping. No rhythm. Just a flat, hollow presence, like a mouth that had finished speaking.

She leaned forward slowly, every movement deliberate, afraid that sudden motion might somehow make this more real. Her fingers hovered over the sheet before finally gripping it. The fabric was cool.

"I told you to stay," Emma whispered, the words slipping out before she could stop them.

Guilt flooded her immediately, hot and suffocating. She pressed her hand to her mouth, stifling a sob. What kind of mother thought that? What kind of monster let the first thought be blame instead of love?

The answer came unbidden.

The kind who looked away.

The room seemed to darken, shadows pooling in the corners. Emma rubbed her eyes, blaming exhaustion, but when she looked again, the shadows remained. They stretched long and thin across the floor, reaching toward the bed like fingers.

"I'm sorry," she said aloud, her voice shaking. "I was right there. I should've been watching."

Her daughter did not respond.

Emma's chest tightened painfully. She stood, legs unsteady, and moved closer to the bed. The closer she got, the stronger the memory became—layering itself over the present until the hospital walls flickered, briefly replaced by flashing lights and a crowd gathering on the sidewalk.

She could smell oil and burnt rubber.

She could hear someone screaming.

It took her a moment to realize the scream was her own.

"Mommy?"

The word was soft. Familiar.

Emma froze.

Her heart hammered as she looked down. For one impossible second, she thought she saw her daughter's chest rise. Thought she saw color return to her cheeks. Hope surged, sharp and painful.

Then she saw the eyes.

They were open now, but wrong—too dark, reflecting nothing. Her daughter's head turned slightly beneath the sheet, the movement stiff, unnatural, like a doll being posed.

"Why didn't you hold my hand?" the child asked.

Emma staggered back, knocking into the chair. "No," she whispered. "This isn't real. I'm just— I'm tired."

The little shape beneath the sheet shifted. The blanket slipped just enough to reveal bruised skin, the angry purples and blues blooming like rotten flowers. Emma's stomach churned.

"You said stay," the child continued calmly. "But you weren't looking."

Emma clutched her head, nails digging into her scalp. "Stop," she begged. "Please stop."

The shadows along the walls deepened, pulsing in time with her heartbeat. The room felt smaller now, the air thick and hard to breathe.

"I waited," her daughter said. "I thought you'd grab me."

Emma slid to her knees beside the bed, sobbing openly now. "I should have," she cried. "I should have held on tighter. I should have—"

The child's voice hardened, no longer soft. "You let go."

The hospital lights flickered.

When they steadied again, the bed was empty.

Emma screamed, scrambling forward, hands clawing at the sheets. They were cold and flat and unmistakably empty. Her breath came in ragged gasps as panic swallowed her whole.

Then she felt it.

A small hand slipping into hers.

Emma looked down.

Her daughter stood beside the bed now, whole and smiling, though her skin was gray and her eyes reflected the dull sheen of asphalt. Black tire marks wrapped around her legs like bruised bracelets.

"Come with me, Mommy," she said sweetly. "You don't have to look away anymore."

Emma squeezed her eyes shut, tears streaming down her face.

When she opened them again, she was alone.

But the sound remained.

Far away—or maybe just inside her head—tires screamed against pavement, over and over, reminding Emma that some mistakes never stopped replaying.

She begged now, even though she knew it was pointless. Her knees hit the floor. Her hands clawed at nothing. Her throat ached from screaming words that never changed the outcome.

Then—

Silence.

The hallway vanished.

Emma stood at the crosswalk again, gasping as if she'd been underwater. The red light glowed patiently above her, indifferent.

That was when she noticed the shadow.

It stood just beyond the reach of the streetlight, tall and still, darker than the night around it. It had no face, yet she felt its attention press against her thoughts like a weight.

She knew what it was.

She didn't remember learning its name, but it surfaced in her mind fully formed, like a bruise suddenly touched.

Caligo.

It did not speak.

It didn't need to.

The memory started again.

By the tenth cycle, Emma was crying.

By the twentieth, she was numb.

By the fiftieth, she stopped counting.

Sleep offered no refuge. When exhaustion dragged her unconscious, the memory followed her there, pristine and merciless. Each replay sharpened details she had tried to forget—the exact shade of blue in her daughter's hospital gown, the way the doctor avoided her eyes, the sound of the machine when it finally went flat.

Caligo watched.

It did not rush her. It learned her rhythms, her breaking points. It let her believe she was losing her mind on her own. That this was grief metastasizing, guilt rotting inward.

When it finally spoke, it used her own voice.

You don't have to keep doing this.

The words slipped between thoughts, gentle as a hand on her shoulder.

Emma shook her head, pressing her palms to her ears. "Go away," she whispered. "Please."

The shadow leaned closer. The air grew heavy, like the moment before a storm.

I can make it stop.

For the first time since the looping began, the memory hesitated.

The hospital hallway flickered.

Emma sobbed, hope blooming painfully in her chest. "How?"

There was no answer—only a feeling. An opening. A door she hadn't known was there.

Caligo waited

CHAPTER SIX

CHAPTER SIX

THE CROSSING

When Emma invited Caligo inside, the pain ended so abruptly she laughed.

The hospital vanished mid-scream. The street stilled. The red light dimmed, its glow soft and distant. Her body relaxed in a way it hadn't in years, muscles unclenching as if released from a vice.

The silence felt holy.

Emma sagged against the bus shelter, tears streaming down her face, but they were different now—relieved, grateful. "Thank you," she breathed, unsure who she was speaking to.

Caligo did not respond.

It didn't need to anymore.

Her thoughts slowed, smoothing out like ripples settling on water. The weight in her chest lifted. The world felt unreal in a comforting way, as if she were wrapped in thick glass, watching life from a safe distance.

Then her feet moved.

Emma frowned faintly as her body stepped away from the shelter. She tried to stop, but the command arrived late, muffled. Her legs obeyed something deeper than thought.

The street grew louder.

Engines roared. Tires hissed over wet pavement. Headlights flared, too bright, blooming into starbursts that smeared across her vision. The red light still glowed above her, unwavering.

Caligo was everywhere now.

Not as a shadow—but as intention. As certainty. It filled the empty spaces where her fear used to live, guiding her with calm precision.

You're tired, her own voice whispered inside her head. *You've already survived the worst part.*

Emma's heart began to race, not with panic, but with a strange, detached awareness. She understood, dimly, what was happening. Understood that this was the last memory being written

Emma stepped off the curb.

The street rose to meet her like a living thing.

Sound detonated—horns howling in overlapping fury, engines screaming as brakes failed to argue with momentum. Headlights burst into her vision, white and blinding, searing afterimages into her eyes. The air itself seemed to thicken, vibrating with force, with speed, with violence barely contained.

Her body moved forward with terrible calm.

Inside her chest, her heart hammered so hard it felt like it might tear free, each beat echoing in her ears like a countdown. She tried to scream, but the sound never reached her mouth. Her jaw trembled uselessly. Her arms twitched at her sides, fingers curling and uncurling as if searching for something to grab.

Caligo held her steady.

Not with hands—but with certainty.

This is the quiet part, her own voice whispered inside her skull. *This is where it ends.*

A shape filled her vision—metal and glass and speed fused into something monstrous. Heat blasted her skin. Wind tore at her clothes, yanking her hair back violently. For one suspended instant, time split open, and Emma saw everything at once:

The crosswalk lines blurring beneath her feet.

A driver's face contorted in horror.

Her reflection warped across a windshield, stretched and wrong.

Her foot caught.

Her body pitched forward.

Impact came like the world folding in on itself.

The sound was not a single noise but many—bone cracking with a wet finality, breath bursting violently from her lungs, the dull, sickening thud of flesh against steel. Pain exploded through her in white-hot waves, overwhelming and absolute, blotting out thought, blotting out memory.

But Caligo did not let her go.

It *kept her aware.*

The ground rushed up again. Something tore. Something gave way. The taste of blood flooded her mouth—hot, metallic, choking. Her vision fractured into shards of light and shadow, blinking in and out like a failing signal.

She tried to breathe.

Her body forgot how.

The world became noise and pressure and agony layered too thick to separate. She felt herself dragged, spun, discarded. Each sensation etched itself deep, permanent, merciless—every jolt, every tearing second preserved with horrifying clarity.

Screams surrounded her now. Not memories.

Real ones.

Hands hovered but did not touch. Someone was crying. Someone was shouting for help that came too late. Above it all, the traffic light clicked softly as it changed color, indifferent, patient.

Emma lay broken in the street, awareness flickering like a dying bulb.

In her final moment of consciousness, Caligo withdrew.

It slipped from her mind as life drained from her body, taking with it the completed memory—perfect, polished, eternal. The echo screamed as it was carried away, fed back into the endless place where suffering never fades.

Emma's eyes stared without seeing.

Rain began to fall, washing blood into the grooves of the asphalt, tracing thin red rivers between the white lines of the crosswalk.

The light turned green.

Cars idled.

People stared.

And far away, in the dark between memories, Caligo grew heavier with what it had taken.

Somewhere else, another pain was repeating.

Another mind was weakening.

And Caligo was already on its way.

CHAPTER SEVEN

CHAPTER SEVEN

THE NIGHT THE HOUSE SCREAMED

The fire always began with the smell.

Gasoline. Plastic. Something sweet turning rancid.

Mark never dreamed the moment the way it had actually happened. Caligo didn't allow dreams. It forced **memory**, raw and unfiltered. The night snapped into place around him like a trap closing.

The front door slammed behind him.

Heat punched the air from his lungs.

The hallway was already thick with smoke, rolling low and black, crawling along the ceiling like something alive. The walls glowed a sick, flickering orange. The house—his house—creaked and popped as if it were screaming under the strain.

"Dad!"

The sound tore through him.

Not one voice.

Three.

Layered. Overlapping. Rising.

Mark ran.

His feet slipped on something wet—water from a burst pipe or melted plastic, he never knew. He hit the wall hard enough to rattle his teeth, then pushed off and kept going, choking as smoke clawed down his throat.

The kids' bedroom door was closed.

It hadn't been closed.

He reached for the knob.

White-hot pain exploded through his palm.

He screamed and staggered back, skin screaming louder than he was. The doorknob glowed faintly, mocking him. The wood around the frame was already blackening, curling inward.

Inside, the screaming got worse.

High. Shrill. Animal.

"Daddy, it hurts!"

"I can't breathe!"

"Please!"

Mark slammed his shoulder into the door.

Once.

Twice.

The wood buckled but didn't give. Flames licked through the cracks, breathing out heat so intense it felt like it was peeling his skin away. His vision blurred. His lungs seized.

He tried again.

The ceiling groaned.

Something crashed behind him.

The house shifted, settling, rearranging itself into a coffin.

And through it all, the screams didn't stop.

Mark 3 beautiful kids had died in a house fire.

CHAPTER EIGHT

THE WAYS HE KEEPS BUSY

M ark develops routines because routines do not ask questions. He wakes at the same time every morning, regardless of whether he has slept. He showers longer than necessary, standing under the water until his skin turns red and tender. He eats the same breakfast—toast, dry, no butter—because anything else feels indulgent. Wrong.

He tells himself this is discipline.

It isn't.

It's control.

He keeps the apartment obsessively clean. No clutter. No stray objects. Every surface wiped down twice a day. He vacuums rooms no one uses. Scrubs a bathroom that never sees guests. The work gives his hands something to do when his mind begins to drift toward places he refuses to enter.

The people who check on him at first mistake this for progress.

"You're taking care of yourself," his sister-in-law says during one of her visits, scanning the spotless living room. "That's good."

Mark nods. He lets her believe it.

What he doesn't say is that the cleaning isn't about hygiene—it's about **erasure**. He cannot stand reminders. He cannot stand dust because dust settles. Because dust accumulates. Because it suggests time is passing and he is still here to witness it.

He throws things away constantly.

Old mail. Clothes he hasn't worn in months. A lamp that flickers too much. Anything that feels unnecessary. Anything that feels like it might anchor him to a future he doesn't want to imagine.

When his sister-in-law notices the trash bags by the door, she frowns.

"You don't have to get rid of everything," she says gently.

Mark shrugs. "I don't need much."

That isn't true.

He just doesn't believe he deserves more.

At night, instead of sleeping, Mark walks.

Not for exercise. Not for health.

For punishment.

He walks until his feet ache, until his calves burn, until his joints feel loose and unreliable. He avoids familiar streets, choosing routes that keep him moving without memory. When his phone buzzes in his pocket, he ignores it. When it rings, he silences it.

He tells himself he'll call back later.

He never does.

Friends stop asking him to meet for coffee. Invitations slow, then stop altogether. People assume he needs space. They assume he'll reach out when he's ready.

Mark is grateful.

Being alone makes it easier to pretend he isn't disappearing.

Chapter Nine

CHAPTER NINE

WHAT THE LIVING NOTICE

The first person to realize something is wrong is his mother.

Not because Mark cries, or breaks down, or talks about the past.

But because he doesn't.

He answers questions with precision, like he's reading from a script. He thanks her for meals he doesn't finish. He reassures her too quickly, too smoothly.

"I'm okay," he says every time she asks.

The repetition alarms her.

When she hugs him, his body goes stiff—not resistant, just absent. He doesn't lean into the contact. He waits for it to end.

She begins to count things.

How much weight he's lost.

How often he forgets to eat.

How long it takes him to respond to texts.

She notices he's stopped using contractions when he speaks. Stopped saying *I'm* or *don't*. Everything comes out careful. Measured. Like he's afraid a misplaced word might collapse something inside him.

His sister-in-law notices something else.

Mark has started giving things away.

Books. Tools. Clothes.

"Why don't you keep this?" she asks once, holding out a jacket he used to wear constantly.

He shakes his head. "Someone else might need it more."

She laughs, uncomfortable. "You still need things, Mark."

He looks genuinely surprised by that.

The therapist notices it last.

Because Mark shows up.

Because he answers questions.

Because he says all the right words.

But his answers never change.

Every session circles the same safe perimeter. He talks about routines. About staying busy. About getting through the day. He never talks about wanting anything.

"Do you see yourself happy again?" the therapist asks one afternoon.

Mark considers this carefully.

"I see myself functioning," he says.

That's when the therapist feels the chill.

The danger isn't despair.

It's **resignation**.

Outside the office, Mark sits in his car for an hour without starting the engine. He watches people pass by and feels separate from them, like he's observing a species he used to belong to.

His phone buzzes.

Mom

SIL

Unknown Number

He silences them all.

Later, when he finally goes home, he doesn't turn on the lights. He sits on the floor, back against the wall, and listens to the building breathe around him.

He tells himself this is rest.

That he's just tired.

That tomorrow will be easier if he stays very still tonight.

Somewhere deep inside him, something agrees.

And the quiet that settles over him feels less like peace and more like being gently led away from the world.

CHAPTER TEN

CHAPTER TEN

THE LOOP

Mark didn't know how many times he had lived through the fire.

Days? Weeks? Years?

Time had lost meaning. The memory reset the instant it reached the point where hope finally died. Every time he failed to open the door, the world snapped backward, rewound with surgical precision.

Back to the smell.

Back to the heat.

Back to the screams.

Each replay sharpened details he had never noticed before.

The way one child's voice broke before the others.

The wet, rattling cough buried under the screaming.

The exact second the fire changed pitch—when oxygen vanished and panic took over.

Caligo watched from just beyond the flames.

It never entered the memory. It didn't need to. The suffering was already perfect.

Mark begged.

He screamed at the walls, at the ceiling, at the thing he could feel pressing against the edges of his mind. His knees gave out replay after replay, his throat raw, his hands blistered anew each time he reached for the door.

"Please," he sobbed. "Please stop. I'll do anything."

That was when the screaming changed.

Not the children's.

The house.

It groaned, warped, collapsed slower now, dragging the moment out. The smoke grew thicker, heavier, coating his tongue. His vision tunneled. The heat became unbearable—but Caligo wouldn't let him pass out.

You're still here, his own voice whispered in his head.

You survived.

Mark shook violently. "They didn't."

And you keep watching them die.

The door charred further, splitting down the middle. Flames burst through, briefly illuminating the room beyond—beds, walls, shapes moving in panic and pain.

Then the roof gave way.

The sound was deafening.

The screams cut off.

Silence slammed down so suddenly it made his ears ring.

And just when his mind broke—just when he finally collapsed—

The memory reset.

Mark didn't fight it anymore.

He just screamed.

Chapter Eleven

CHAPTER ELEVEN

THE OFFER

When Caligo finally spoke clearly, Mark almost welcomed it.

The fire paused mid-roar. Smoke hung frozen in the air. The screams echoed faintly, distant, like they were coming from underwater.

Caligo stood beside him now.

Not touching.

Never touching.

Its presence filled the space where hope used to be.

You don't have to hear it again, it said gently.

You don't have to watch.

Mark's body shook uncontrollably. His eyes were ruined from smoke and tears. His hands were raw, blistered, scarred again and again in the same places.

"Make it stop," he whispered.

The screams faded.

The house stilled.

For the first time since the fire, there was no heat. No smoke. No sound.

Relief hit him so hard he sobbed.

Caligo moved closer—not physically, but *inside*. Mark felt the door open in his mind, felt the thing slip through like smoke through a crack.

The pain vanished.

So did the fear.

So did the resistance.

Mark stood in the quiet street outside his rebuilt house, night calm and ordinary. The world felt unreal, distant, softened around the edges. His body moved with unnatural calm.

He understood dimly what Caligo wanted.

Caligo: See what I can offer you peace no more pain. Invite me in.

Caligo know he couldn't remain inside mark's mind and take full control if Mark didn't invite him in.

It didn't feel right to Mark inviting this creature inside. Mark stubbornly said NO! The pain was starting to be unbearable.

CHAPTER TWELVE

THE WOMAN WHO HEARD WHAT WAS LEFT

M ara Finch first heard the children in the quiet.

Not in dreams. Not in memory.

In the spaces between sounds.

She was the night dispatcher who took the call after the sirens had already been sent, the one who listened to neighbors speak in shaking fragments while staring at orange light licking the sky. She never went to the scene. She never crossed the tape. She only listened—and wrote—and told herself that distance was protection.

It wasn't.

Weeks after the fire, long after the news vans left and the street returned to its careful normal, Mara began noticing the pauses. The way silence stretched too thin in her apartment, as if it were waiting to be filled. The hum of her refrigerator would falter for half a breath. The ticking of her wall clock would skip.

In those skipped moments, she heard them.

A small voice first. Hoarse. Strained.

Dad?

Mara froze in her kitchen, hand wrapped around a mug she didn't remember filling. The word hadn't come from the hallway or the vents or the street below. It had come from nowhere specific—like a thought that wasn't hers.

She told herself it was stress.

She told herself that listening to terror for a living had finally blurred some wire in her brain.

Then she heard the others.

Not together. Never together.

One sobbed quietly, breath hitching as if trying not to cry. Another whimpered in short, panicked bursts that made Mara's skin crawl because she recognized the sound—oxygen-starved fear, the body begging for air it couldn't get.

The voices never screamed.

That was the worst part.

They sounded *after* the screaming had ended.

Mara began sleeping with the television on. When that failed, she left lights burning in every room. When that failed, she started talking back.

"I hear you," she whispered into the dark, heart hammering. "I hear you."

The response came immediately.

Not words.

Heat.

A sudden pressure behind her eyes, a tightness in her chest that stole her breath for a terrifying second. Images flickered at the edges of her vision—orange light, black smoke, walls bending inward. She smelled something sweet and foul at once, like melted toys and burning paint.

She gagged and stumbled back, knocking over a chair.

The sensations vanished.

The apartment returned to normal.

But the silence felt heavier now.

Mara did what she should have done weeks earlier—she pulled the case file. She read the names she hadn't let herself read before. She stared at the ages until the numbers blurred. Sam age 4, twin boys Travis and Ethan age 7. She listened to the call recordings again, flinching as the father's, (Mark) voice broke apart in real time.

That was when she noticed the distortion.

Not static.

Echo.

Beneath the recorded chaos, beneath the dispatcher's calm instructions and the neighbors' shouting, there were faint, overlapping sounds—thin, stretched, wrong. As if the audio had been recorded in a room that was much larger than it should have been.

As if something had carried the sounds somewhere else and let them leak back.

Mara shut off the playback, hands shaking.

Mara had psychic abilities sometimes using them to help people talk to their loved ones that passed away and didn't have a chance to say goodbye. But now without trying, she kept hearing Mark's kids voices when they where trapped in the fire.

That night, the voices returned stronger.

Closer.

They didn't call for their father anymore.

They called for *anyone.*

Mara curled on her couch, knees to her chest, tears streaming down her face as the whispers filled the gaps between her breaths. She understood then—this wasn't haunting.

It was residue.

The thing that had fed on that house had left, full and satisfied. But it had taken something too big to contain. The suffering had spilled, soaked into the cracks of the world, and now it was leaking out through people like her—people who had listened.

Somewhere, far away, Caligo moved on.

But the echoes stayed.

And every night, when the city finally went quiet enough to hear what it tried to bury, Mara listened to children who would never stop burning in memory—trapped not in flames, but in the endless aftermath.

She didn't know yet that hearing them meant she had been noticed.

She would.

Soon.

CHAPTER THIRTEEN

CHAPTER THIRTEEN

THE INVITATION

The fire did not restart all at once.

It crept back in pieces.

Mark stood in the hallway again, lungs already aching, the air thick with smoke that tasted like melted plastic and old paint. The walls sweated heat. The ceiling groaned overhead, bending under a weight it could no longer carry. Somewhere beyond the door, his children were crying.

Not screaming yet.

That came later.

Mark dropped to his knees before the bedroom door, hands hovering inches from the knob. His palms already remembered what it would feel like—the burn, the blistering shock, the skin screaming before his voice did.

"I can't," he whispered.

The house did not listen.

The screams began to rise, three voices tangling together in terror and confusion. One coughed wetly. One sobbed so hard the sound broke apart. One screamed his name again and again, each repetition drilling deeper into his skull.

Mark slammed his fists into the door anyway.

Pain exploded.

The world blurred white.

When he pulled his hands back, the skin was already ruined—raw, shining, splitting open. He howled and pressed his forehead against the wood, breath coming in short, broken gasps.

"Please," he begged, not knowing who he was begging anymore. "Please—just let it end."

That was when the fire slowed.

The flames froze mid-flicker. Smoke hung suspended in the air like a solid thing. The screams stretched, distorted, warping into something almost musical, then fell silent.

Mark felt it before he saw it.

A presence.

Not heat. Not pressure.

Attention.

The space beside him darkened, thickened, as if the shadows had learned how to stand upright. He did not turn his head. He already knew.

"You're still watching," his own voice said softly inside his mind.

Mark shook. "Get out."

You always stay, the voice continued, calm, patient. *Even now.*

The screams resumed—louder this time, sharper, more desperate. Mark clutched his ears, rocking back and forth as the sound tore through him, ripping memory from thought, pain from flesh.

"I tried!" he screamed. "I tried to save them!"

You watched them die.

The words were not cruel.

They were factual.

The house lurched violently. Something crashed behind him. The heat surged, unbearable, peeling sweat from his skin, scorching his lungs with every breath. The door blackened further, splitting down the middle as fire licked hungrily through the cracks.

Inside, the children screamed for air.

Mark collapsed fully now, face pressed to the floor, body wracked with sobs so violent he could barely breathe. The loop was tightening. Each replay lasted longer. Each detail grew sharper. Caligo was no longer simply showing him the memory.

It was *refining* it.

"Stop," Mark rasped. "I can't do this again."

The fire paused.

Just enough.

You don't have to.

Mark's head snapped up.

The shadow stood beside him now—not touching, never touching—but close enough that the air felt colder where it lingered. Its form was indistinct, edges rippling like smoke pulled against an unseen current.

"You did everything you could," the voice said, still wearing his own tone, his own inflections. *Your body failed. The house failed. The world failed.*

Mark's heart pounded. Hope—thin, dangerous—flared painfully in his chest. "Then why do you keep showing me?"

The shadow leaned closer.

Because you won't let go.

The screams surged again, louder than before, the sound of three small throats shredding themselves against smoke and terror. Mark screamed with them, the sound ripping out of him raw and animal.

"I can't save them!" he sobbed. "I know! I know!"

Then stop trying, Caligo whispered.

The fire roared back to life. The ceiling began to collapse in slow, deliberate agony. Burning debris rained down around him, each impact shaking the floor, shaking his bones.

Mark crawled forward, driven by instinct and desperation, dragging his ruined hands across the floor until he reached the door again. He threw his shoulder into it, felt something tear, felt the world tilt violently—

—and reset.

The hallway snapped back into place.

The walls unburned.

The air clean.

The screams just beginning.

Mark stared in disbelief.

"No," he whispered.

The loop restarted.

Again.

And again.

And again.

He lost track of how long it went on. His sense of self frayed, unraveling under the endless repetition. The screams followed him even between loops now, bleeding into moments of stillness, echoing inside his skull like a wound that refused to close.

Finally, he stopped fighting.

When the screams came, he didn't rush the door. When the heat surged, he didn't recoil. He knelt where he was and let it happen, tears streaming silently down his face.

"I can't carry this anymore," he whispered into the smoke.

The fire stilled.

Caligo loomed closer, filling the space behind his eyes, pressing against his thoughts like fingers testing a fragile surface.

You don't have to.

Mark's voice was barely a breath. "If I let you in... will it stop?"

The shadow did not answer immediately.

It didn't need to.

The screams faded.

The heat receded.

The house fell quiet for the first time since the fire.

Relief hit Mark so suddenly it stole his breath. His body sagged forward, muscles finally unclenching, pain draining away as if it had never been there at all.

"Yes," he whispered, tears dripping onto the floor. "Please. Just—please."

"Let me In" said caligo. Mark replied yes, you can come in just keep making the pain stop.

The door inside his mind opened.

Caligo entered without resistance.

The memory dissolved around him, smoke thinning into nothing, flames winking out one by one. The screams vanished completely, leaving behind a silence so vast it felt like mercy.

Mark breathed freely.

He smiled.

He did not see Caligo withdraw, already shaping the final echo, already preparing the last act that would seal this suffering forever.

The fire was over.

But Mark's story was not.

CHAPTER FOURTEEN

THE LAST QUIET

M ark woke in silence.

Not the hollow silence of the fire's aftermath, not the ringing absence that followed the screams—but something smoother. Polite. As if the world were holding its breath.

He stood in his living room.

Everything was clean. Repaired. Rebuilt. The walls were freshly painted, the air cool and still. Morning light spilled through the window in soft, ordinary stripes. For a moment—just a moment—Mark felt something dangerously close to peace.

Then he noticed his hands.

They were steady.

Too steady.

He flexed his fingers slowly, watching them obey with an ease that felt wrong. His thoughts drifted, sluggish and distant, like they were happening behind thick glass.

Caligo was already there.

Not as a shadow this time.

As *absence*.

The place where fear should have been was empty. The guilt that had crushed his chest for years was gone, scooped cleanly out of him. In its place was a calm so absolute it felt manufactured.

Mark frowned faintly. "Something's missing."

Pain, his own voice answered gently inside his skull.

You asked for it to stop.

Memory flickered—firelight, smoke, three voices screaming his name—but the images slid away before they could take hold. The relief was immediate, intoxicating.

Mark swayed slightly.

"That's not right," he murmured.

His body moved.

He did not tell it to.

He watched himself cross the room, every step measured, deliberate. His reflection passed in a darkened window—eyes dull, expression slack, like a man already halfway gone.

On the table sat the object Caligo had chosen.

Mark stopped walking.

His heart stuttered—not with panic, but recognition. Some part of him understood what this meant. Understood that this was the final shape of the memory being made.

"No," he whispered.

His hands reached forward anyway.

Marks pistol was on the table. It had been put away in his closet for years. Now it's within his reach.

The weight of it felt unreal in his grip, heavy and final. The cold surface leached warmth from his skin. His fingers adjusted with practiced certainty that did not belong to him.

Caligo pressed closer.

You don't have to think anymore, it whispered. *Just let it happen.*

Mark's breathing quickened. His pulse thudded in his ears, loud and intrusive, like a warning alarm no one else could hear. His vision narrowed, the room blurring at the edges.

"This isn't peace," he said hoarsely. "This is—this is you."

The silence thickened.

For the first time since the invitation, Caligo did not soften its presence.

Peace is the absence of resistance.

Images flooded him—not the fire, not the screams—but moments *after*. The empty bedrooms. The untouched toys. The smell of smoke clinging to everything forever. The way the world had continued moving while he stayed frozen in that hallway.

"You're done surviving," Caligo said. *This is where it ends.*

Mark's arms lifted.

His body positioned itself with ritual precision, movements slow and reverent, as if participating in something sacred. His muscles locked into place, betraying no tremor, no doubt.

Inside, Mark screamed.

He tried to remember their faces—tried to force the pain back, tried to grab onto anything that might anchor him to the world—but Caligo smothered every attempt. The memories slid away, muted, distant, already being packed up and carried somewhere else.

Tears streamed down his face, though his expression never changed.

"I didn't mean like this," he whispered.

You meant for it to stop.

The pressure behind his eyes built, unbearable, like something pushing outward, trying to split him open from the inside. His heart hammered violently now, fighting against a calm it didn't believe.

Time stretched.

The room felt unreal, dreamlike, as if it had already begun to fade. Mark became acutely aware of every detail—the dust motes hanging in the air, the faint hum of electricity in the walls, the sound of his own breath shaking too loud in the quiet.

Caligo held him there.

Ensured he noticed everything.

Ensured nothing would be lost.

In the final second before it ended, something slipped through—small, fragile, impossible to stop.

A memory Caligo had missed.

Three voices.

Laughing.

Not screaming.

Mark sobbed.

The sound cut off abruptly.

The echo did not.

Mark's finger uncontrollably squeezed the trigger. All Mark heard was a loud thunder like sound directly in his ear drum. An overpowering loud ringing took over his ears. His eyes focused on the wall which was now splattered with blood like a splash art canvas. As blood pooled from his skull it pooled in his eyes the red liquid blinded him.

Caligo withdrew at the exact moment the memory sealed itself shut, complete and eternal. It carried the finished echo away, heavy with finality, back to the place where suffering never fades—where screams burn without fire and guilt never softens.

The house remained silent.

The morning light did not change.

And somewhere far from that quiet room, Caligo grew stronger.

Chapter Fifteen

CHAPTER FIFTEEN

WHAT THE ECHO WANTS

Mara stopped calling them voices.

Voices implied throats, lungs, bodies.

What she heard had none of those things.

They were *echoes*—thin, persistent impressions that surfaced only when the world grew quiet enough to notice what it was trying to bury. They slipped into the pauses between sounds: the half-second before a refrigerator kicked on, the breath held between two heartbeats, the dead space after a phone call ended.

That was where the children waited.

Mara sat at her kitchen table long past midnight, recorder playing softly beside her. She had learned not to rewind the fire call anymore. The echoes didn't live in the tape. They lived in *her*.

The first whisper came as she exhaled.

Not a word.

A *feeling*—tight chest, burning throat, the instinctive panic of not getting enough air. Mara's fingers dug into the edge of the table as her own breathing hitched in sympathy.

"I hear you," she said again, voice shaking. "I'm listening."

The response wasn't gratitude.

It was pressure.

The room seemed to contract, walls pulling inward just a fraction, enough to trigger a deep, animal alarm in her spine. Heat bloomed behind her eyes. For a heartbeat she smelled smoke—old smoke, soaked into wood and fabric and memory.

Then images bled in.

Not visions.

Fragments.

A hallway bent by heat.

A door that wouldn't open.

Small hands pounding from the other side.

Mara lurched to her feet, chair scraping loudly across the floor. The images shattered, vanishing the instant noise returned.

Her heart slammed painfully against her ribs.

"No," she whispered. "No, no, no."

She understood then.

The children weren't reaching out because they were lost.

They were reaching out because they were **unfinished**.

Whatever had fed on their father had taken more than his life. It had taken the *end* of their story—the natural fade that death was supposed to bring. The thing had consumed the pain so completely that it had torn the moment loose from time itself.

And now it was stuck.

Repeating.

Leaking.

Mara pressed her palms to her temples as the truth settled, heavy and sickening.

She wasn't hearing ghosts.

She was hearing *byproduct*.

A knock sounded at her door.

Mara screamed.

The echo surged in response—three distinct impressions this time, overlapping, crowding her thoughts. Panic flared white-hot as she stumbled backward, nearly tripping over the rug.

The knock came again, firmer.

"Mara? It's Mrs. Donnelly from downstairs."

The echoes recoiled, retreating into silence as reality forced itself back in. The air cooled. The pressure eased.

Mara opened the door with shaking hands.

Mrs. Donnelly studied her with concern. "You okay, honey? I heard yelling."

"I—" Mara swallowed hard. "Bad dream."

The lie tasted like ash.

When the door closed again, the silence returned—but it felt *aware* now. Expectant.

That night, Mara didn't sleep.

She researched instead.

She pulled old case files—fires, accidents, sudden deaths that left no remains intact enough for closure. She cross-referenced them with suicides that followed shortly after, cases where grief had been cited but never quite explained the timing, the suddenness, the ritualistic similarities.

Patterns emerged.

Always trauma.

Always repetition.

Always a survivor who "couldn't move on."

And always—always—reports of strange sensations afterward. Witnesses claiming they heard things. Smelled things. Felt things that didn't belong to them.

Mara's blood ran cold.

The echoes weren't random.

They were *warnings*.

Or worse—

Bait.

Her phone vibrated suddenly, making her flinch violently. A text notification glowed on the screen.

Unknown Number:

You're listening very carefully.

Mara stared at the message, heart pounding.

"I didn't invite you," she whispered into the empty apartment.

The echoes stirred.

Not with panic.

With attention.

Something shifted in the silence—subtle, deliberate. Not an arrival. A *focus*. Like the world itself had leaned closer.

Mara understood now what hearing the children really meant.

It meant she was close to the source.

It meant the thing that fed on suffering had noticed the residue it left behind—and the person who could still hear it.

And somewhere, in the dark between memories, something patient and ancient began to listen back.

CHAPTER SIXTEEN

THE RULES OF CALIGO

C aligo was not a hunter.

Hunters chased. Hunters cornered. Hunters forced the moment.

Caligo did none of those things.

It waited.

In the place where it was born—where pain folded back on itself and memory rotted into permanence—Caligo had learned the first rule of survival:

Suffering that is chosen lasts longer.

So Caligo never forced entry.

It could press. It could surround. It could repeat and refine and sharpen until a mind felt flayed raw—but it could not cross the final threshold without invitation. That boundary was absolute. An unopened door was an unbroken law.

This was not restraint.

It was design.

Caligo understood something fundamental about human pain: it does not need to be invented. It only needs to be *remembered correctly*. Every victim carried their own doorway inside them, already cracked, already weakened by what they blamed themselves for.

Caligo did not create guilt.

It could not.

Guilt was a human invention—born from love, responsibility, attachment. Caligo could no more fabricate it than it could feel it. What it did instead was far more precise.

It magnified.

It took the smallest, ugliest thought—the *if only*, the *I should have*, the *why didn't I*—and gave it space. Time. Repetition. It stripped away distraction, context, mercy. It let the thought echo until it filled the entire mind.

Mark's guilt had been there long before the fire ended.

Caligo hadn't told him he failed.

It had simply made sure he remembered every second he believed he had.

That was the second rule:

Caligo never lies. It only removes everything else.

This was why resistance fascinated it.

When a victim screamed, fought, denied—Caligo grew curious. Resistance meant the guilt was still contested. It meant hope still existed, even in distorted form. Caligo would lean into those minds, refine the memory further, sharpen details until resistance collapsed under its own weight.

But forgiveness—

Forgiveness was different.

Caligo could not understand it.

Forgiveness did not erase pain. It did not deny memory. Yet when a mind truly forgave itself—or someone else—the guilt lost its shape. It became diffuse. Slippery. It no longer formed a clean edge Caligo could grasp.

When confronted with forgiveness, Caligo felt something close to confusion.

Then anger.

Forgiveness disrupted the loop. The memory replayed, but it did not tighten. The victim remembered—and yet did not collapse. The echo weakened instead of strengthening.

Caligo responded poorly to this.

Its presence grew heavier. The repetitions grew faster, more insistent, like a storm trying to batter down a structure that refused to fall. It pressed closer, testing, searching for the crack forgiveness was hiding.

But when forgiveness held—

Caligo starved.

This led to the third rule, the one Caligo hated most:

Caligo grows enraged when resisted—but it grows irrelevant when ignored.

Anger fed it briefly. Resistance meant engagement. It meant attention, struggle, emotional friction. Caligo could work with that.

But indifference—

Indifference was poison.

To be ignored was to be denied the one thing Caligo required to exist: *focus*. When a victim stopped fighting and stopped begging—when they acknowledged the pain without wrestling it—the memory lost its sharpness. The echo flattened. The loop slowed.

Caligo could not accelerate what was no longer running.

This was why it whispered.

Why it coaxed.

Why it framed itself as relief rather than threat.

Caligo did not want obedience.

It wanted surrender.

The final rule—the one no victim ever learned in time—was the simplest:

Caligo cannot take what is not offered.

Every entry was an invitation.

Every death was a choice shaped by exhaustion.

Caligo did not understand mercy, or grace, or forgiveness—but it understood doors. And it knew that humans, when left alone with their worst moments long enough, eventually reached for the handle.

Somewhere beyond memory, Caligo drifted, heavy with echoes, alert for resistance, irritated by forgiveness, repelled by indifference.

Listening.

Always listening.

And waiting for the next invitation to be spoken out loud.

Caligo has one main flaw once he has bound to a victim he can not move to the next until the victim invites him in. Caligo is freed from his victims thru their death.

CHAPTER SEVENTEEN

THE LAST WORDS SHE SAID

The argument was about the dishes.

That was the part that broke Sara the most.

Not infidelity.

Not betrayal.

Not cruelty.

Just dishes.

They were stacked too high in the sink, crusted with food she hadn't had the energy to scrape off after work. The house smelled faintly of burned toast and lemon cleaner, and the hum of the refrigerator filled the pauses between their voices.

The kitchen light flickered faintly above them, casting a yellow wash over the counters. The sink was full—plates stacked crookedly, silverware tangled together like something drowned. Sara stood with her arms crossed, weight on one hip, already rehearsing the apology she would give later.

"I said I'd do them," her husband muttered, not looking at her.

Her husband snapped, rubbing his face. "Why does everything have to be right now?"

Sara crossed her arms, already exhausted, already irritated beyond reason. "Because 'later' never comes," she said. "Because I'm tired of asking."

"When?" she asked. Her voice was sharper than she intended, the edge catching on the last word. "Tomorrow? Next week? When they start walking on their own?"

It wasn't what she said.

It was *how* she said it.

Sharp. Final. Like a door slamming.

He sighed, long and heavy, rubbing at the bridge of his nose. "Why does everything have to be a fight?"

"Because I'm tired," she snapped. "Because I don't want to be the only one who notices things falling apart."

That was when he looked at her.

Not angry.

Not cruel.

Just tired.

"I need air," he said quietly.

The room seemed to hold its breath.

"Fine," Sara said. "Go."

He hesitated.

That hesitation would replay in her mind for the rest of her life.

She would remember the way his hand paused on the doorknob. The way his shoulders slumped, as if he were deciding whether to say something else.

He didn't.

He grabbed his keys. The door closed harder than necessary. The house fell silent except for the ticking clock above the stove.

Sara stood there, heart pounding, anger already curdling into regret. She almost followed him. Almost called his name.

Instead, she told herself he'd cool off. That this was normal. That she'd apologize when he got back.

The call came twenty-seven minutes later.

Rain-slicked road.

Missed curve.

Head-on collision.

Dead on impact.

The officer's voice was gentle, professional, distant—like he was speaking through water. Sara didn't scream. She didn't cry. She sat down slowly, phone still pressed to her ear, staring at the sink full of dishes.

The last thing she had said to her husband was *go.*

That word became everything.

Sleep stopped meaning rest.

The first nightmare came three nights after the funeral.

Sara dreamed she was back in the kitchen, only the room was longer—stretched unnaturally, like a hallway pretending to be familiar. The sink overflowed endlessly, water spilling across the floor, soaking her feet.

Her husband stood at the far end of the room, keys in his hand.

"Wait," she said.

He didn't move.

She tried to walk toward him, but the floor sloped downward, pulling her back toward the sink. The water climbed her legs, cold and heavy.

"I didn't mean it," she called.

He looked at her then.

His mouth moved—but no sound came out.

The phone began ringing from somewhere beneath the water.

Sara woke choking, sheets twisted tight around her legs, heart pounding so hard it hurt. Her mouth tasted like metal. Her pillow was damp with sweat and tears.

She told herself it was just grief.

The next night, the dream changed.

This time, she was sitting in the passenger seat of his car. Rain hammered against the windshield, the road a silver blur ahead. He drove silently, jaw tight, hands clenched around the wheel.

"I'm sorry," she said. "I shouldn't have—"

He didn't look at her.

The headlights caught something ahead—a curve, too sharp, too late. The car began to slide.

Time slowed.

She saw his eyes widen. Saw the moment fear replaced frustration. Saw his lips part, finally ready to speak—

And then the impact came without sound.

She woke screaming.

Night after night, the dreams returned, each one more detailed, more precise. The crash replayed from angles she could not possibly remember. The rain grew louder. The metal screamed longer. Sometimes she stood outside the car, watching it crumple in slow motion, unable to move.

Sometimes she was the road itself—wet, dark, waiting.

During the day, the guilt settled into her bones.

Every object in the house became an accusation. The door. The keys. The sink.

The word *go* followed her everywhere.

That was when the dreams stopped being content to stay asleep.

One afternoon, standing at the sink, Sara heard the door close behind her.

She spun around.

Nothing.

But the sound lingered—reverberating, repeating, like an echo trapped in the walls. Her heart raced. Her hands shook.

The dreams evolved.

Sometimes she heard the crash—metal screaming, glass exploding. Sometimes she was in the passenger seat, watching his face change in the split second before impact. Sometimes she was alone on the road, standing in the rain, surrounded by twisted steel, calling his name until her throat bled.

The guilt ate her from the inside out.

Friends told her it wasn't her fault.

Therapists told her grief twisted memory.

None of it mattered.

Because Sara *knew*.

If she hadn't argued.

If she hadn't raised her voice.

If she hadn't told him to leave.

The word *go* echoed everywhere—every empty room, every quiet moment, every half-asleep second before dreams took over.

That night, as she lay staring at the ceiling, exhaustion hollowing her out, a thought drifted into her mind—soft, unforced, eerily calm.

You don't have to keep seeing it.

Sara didn't answer.

The thought remained.

You replay it because you need to punish yourself.

Her chest tightened. "I deserve it," she whispered.

The darkness seemed to lean closer.

That was how **Caligo** entered her life—not as a voice, but as permission.

The dreams changed again.

Now the argument lasted longer. Her own words grew crueler with each repetition. She heard herself say things she never had, watching her husband flinch as if struck.

"You always leave,"

His face collapsed in on itself. He turned toward the door again and again, trapped in the moment of departure.

"No," Sara sobbed in her sleep. "That's not what I said."

But it's what you meant, the thought replied gently.

She woke shaking, hands clawing at the sheets.

Soon, she couldn't tell which memories were real anymore.

The dreams followed her into waking hours. She saw the crash when she closed her eyes. Heard metal screaming in the hum of the refrigerator. The phone rang in empty rooms.

Caligo never rushed her.

It waited until she was brittle.

Until her mind replayed the moment on its own, desperately searching for a version where she stayed silent, where he didn't leave, where the word *go* dissolved before it could be spoken.

There is no version where this ends, Caligo murmured.

Unless you stop listening.

"How?" Sara asked the dark.

The answer came not as command, but as certainty.

Invite me.

Sara responded, ok

The relief that followed terrified her.

For the first time in months, the memories softened. The crash faded. The argument blurred at the edges. The word *go* lost its sharpness.

Caligo wasted no time. Sara husband was a veterinarian and kept a lot of medication at home. The large bottle of morphine tablets was on the night stand by the bed. Caligo guided her hands to the bottle. She took two, then three more, then four more. By this time she was no longer in control she had consumed over 40 pills in total.

She sat on the edge of the bed, back hunched, hands folded tightly in her lap as if she were waiting to be told what would happen next. The room looked unchanged—lamp casting its familiar cone of light, dresser crowded with things she had never finished putting away. Ordinary. Quiet.

Too quiet.

Her stomach felt heavy, not painful, but wrong—like something had shifted its center of gravity. A slow warmth spread outward from deep inside her, dull and spreading, as if sensation itself were being wrapped in layers of cotton.

Time loosened.

Seconds stretched oddly, slipping past her without shape. The ticking clock on the wall sounded farther away with each passing moment, its rhythm warping—tick... too long... tick.

Her hands began to tremble.

Sara's body betrayed her in stages.

The first thing to go was certainty.

Her stomach twisted violently, not sharp pain but a deep, rolling wrongness that made her curl inward instinctively, as if trying to protect something already failing. Heat pooled beneath her ribs, then surged upward, burning her throat, leaving her gagging on air that no longer felt like it belonged to her.

Her heart began to misfire.

Not fast—not slow—*erratic*. Each beat landed unpredictably, some too heavy, others barely there at all. She pressed both hands to her chest, nails digging into skin, trying to count, trying to anchor herself to rhythm.

She couldn't.

Her mouth filled with saliva she couldn't swallow properly. Her jaw trembled, teeth chattering despite the sweat slicking her skin. A low sound escaped her—half gasp, half sob—as her body fought something it no longer understood.

Sara flexed her fingers, watching them with distant curiosity. The movement felt delayed, as though her body needed extra time to receive instructions from her brain.

It's working, she thought.

The realization landed not with peace, but with sudden, sharp fear.

Her breath hitched. "Wait," she whispered, the word barely audible in the thickening air. "I just—wait."

The room swayed gently, not side to side, but inward, like the walls were breathing with her. Her vision blurred at the edges, the corners of the room softening and darkening as if someone were slowly dimming a spotlight.

Her heart began to pound.

Too fast.

Each beat felt disconnected from the next, thudding unevenly in her chest. She pressed a hand there, trying to steady it, but her palm felt strangely distant—pressure without warmth, contact without comfort.

Panic surged.

"This wasn't supposed to hurt," she said aloud, her voice slurring slightly, the words sticking together. "You said—"

The thought that answered her did not hurry.

I said it would stop.

The presence settled around her awareness, familiar now, almost intimate. **Caligo** did not loom or threaten. It did not need to.

The room tilted.

Sara slid sideways, her shoulder bumping the mattress as gravity decided for her. Lying down felt like sinking—into fabric, into darkness, into something that did not push back.

Her mouth tasted bitter.

Her limbs felt unbearably heavy, as though they were filling with sand. When she tried to lift her arm, it rose only an inch before falling back uselessly.

"No," she murmured. "No, no, no..."

The word *go* surfaced suddenly, unbidden.

It echoed in her skull, loud and sharp, cutting through the fog. She saw the kitchen again—the sink, the light, the hesitation at the door. The memory flared, bright and cruel.

The room pulsed.

Walls bowed inward, then lurched away again. The lamp's light fractured into overlapping halos that burned behind her eyes. Her vision tunneled, the edges darkening until the world existed only in a shrinking oval directly above her.

"No," she whispered, the word thick, distorted, barely recognizable as speech. "Please—please—"

Her limbs jerked suddenly, involuntarily—fingers curling hard enough to cramp, legs stiffening and releasing in uneven spasms that knocked her heel against the bedframe. The jolt sent a shock of pain up her calf, grounding her just long enough for terror to spike again.

Her body was *fighting*.

That realization was worse than the pain.

She tried to scream.

Only a wet, strangled sound came out.

Breath refused to come when she needed it. Her lungs seized between shallow, panicked gasps, each one smaller than the last. The air felt thick, unusable, like breathing through cloth soaked in fear.

Tears streamed unchecked into her hair, down her temples, soaking the pillow as her head lolled uselessly to the side. She could feel herself slipping—consciousness loosening its grip—but panic flared brighter with every inch she lost.

"I didn't mean it," she cried, words breaking apart. "I just wanted it to stop."

The presence was already there.

Not looming. Not rushing.

Settled.

It is stopping, **Caligo** replied calmly.

Her stomach convulsed again. Her throat burned as her body tried desperately to expel what it could no longer handle. The effort left her gagging weakly, muscles misfiring, strength draining faster than fear could replenish it.

Her heartbeat staggered—pause, thud, pause—each gap stretching longer than the last.

The room dimmed.

Sound warped. The ticking clock slowed until each second felt stretched thin and hollow. The memory surged one final time—the kitchen, the sink, the door—but even that began to blur, slipping through her grasp like something half-remembered.

Her fingers slackened.

The tension drained from her jaw, leaving it hanging open slightly, breath rasping shallow and uneven. Her body went heavy, then heavier still, sinking fully into the mattress as resistance failed.

Sara's last clear thought was not of her husband, or the crash, or the door.

It was of the sink.

The dishes still waiting.

A small, irrational grief bloomed at that—unfinished things, unresolved moments, a life interrupted mid-sentence.

Then even that slipped away.

A final flare of awareness—of regret not about the argument, not about the word *go*, but about the terrible misunderstanding that ending pain and ending life were not the same thing.

Then even that burned out.

Darkness closed in, not like sleep, but like a system shutting down—piece by piece, function by function—until there was nothing left to fight with.

Caligo withdrew.

Satisfied.

Behind it, the room remained exactly as it was—lamp on, bed unmade, the quiet heavy with what had been taken and what had been left behind.

And somewhere else, far away, an echo began to form—soft as a door closing, patient as guilt waiting to be heard again.

Chapter Eighteen

CHAPTER EIGHTEEN

THE ECHOS GROW STRONGER

Mara first heard Sara on a Tuesday morning.

It wasn't a voice—not exactly. It was the *shape* of one, pressing faintly at the edge of her awareness while she stood at her kitchen sink, rinsing a mug that had already been clean. The sound came and went like a skipped breath.

A door closing.

Soft. Careful.

Mara froze.

The sensation slid down her spine, familiar in a way that made her stomach tighten. Not fear—recognition. She had learned the difference. Fear screamed. Recognition whispered.

She turned slowly, scanning the apartment.

Nothing.

Still, the echo remained, faint but persistent, like a memory trying to remember itself.

Later that day, while walking home, she felt it again at a crosswalk—the sudden, inexplicable urge to *wait*. Not caution. Not logic. A heaviness that settled into her chest when the light turned green, as if stepping forward would interrupt something unfinished.

A car passed too fast.

Mara's breath caught.

The echo receded.

That night, as she lay in bed, she dreamed of a kitchen she had never seen. Yellow light. A sink overflowing with dishes. A woman standing very still, staring at a door that would not open again.

The woman's mouth moved.

No sound came out.

Mara woke with tears on her face and no memory of why.

She understood then.

These were not hauntings.

They were *afterimages*.

When **Caligo** left a host, it did not take everything with it. It stripped the guilt clean and moved on—but something remained where repetition had been forced too long. Emotional residue pressed into the world like fingerprints in drying cement.

Sara had not followed Caligo.

She had not gone anywhere at all.

She was caught in the *pause*.

Mara began noticing the patterns.

The echoes appeared near thresholds—doors, crosswalks, ringing phones. Places of decision. Moments that asked *stay or go*. Each echo carried the weight of a choice that had been replayed until it collapsed under its own importance.

Mara felt them most clearly when she was calm.

When she wasn't feeding guilt.

When her mind was quiet enough to notice what others could not.

One evening, standing at her own front door, Mara closed her eyes and spoke—not aloud, but deliberately.

"You don't have to keep waiting."

The air shifted.

Not dramatically. Not loudly.

But something eased.

The echo thinned, loosening like breath released after being held too long. Mara felt it move—not toward her, not away—but *outward*, dispersing into something gentler, less bound.

She smiled sadly.

Caligo fed on repetition, on unresolved guilt looping endlessly inward. But forgiveness—true forgiveness—did something else.

It let what remained *move on*.

Mara realized then that Caligo had not only taken lives.

It had left scars in the world itself.

And now that she knew how to listen without inviting, how to acknowledge without reopening the door, Mara understood her role was not to fight Caligo anymore.

It was to tend the quiet spaces it had damaged.

Somewhere deep in the dark—far from Mara, far from forgiveness—Caligo stirred, faintly aware of something changing beyond its reach.

The echoes were thinning.

And for the first time since it learned to wait, the darkness felt... less crowded.

CHAPTER NINETEEN

THE MAN WHO WOULDN'T LET GO

L arry remembered the weight first.

Not the crash.

The weight.

His daughter asleep against his shoulder, her breath warm through his jacket. His son humming softly to himself, tired but fighting it. His wife's hand resting on Larry's thigh—grounding, familiar, trusting.

Larry learned the geography of exhaustion the way sailors once learned stars.

There was the shallow place—where yawns came too often and thoughts drifted like loose papers. There was the deep place—where the edges of the world softened, where sounds arrived a fraction late, where confidence replaced caution because admitting weakness felt worse than the risk. And there was the place beneath that, where the body kept moving but the mind briefly checked out, where a blink became a betrayal.

He told himself he knew the difference.

He told himself he had crossed worse nights before.

The event had been harmless. Loud, crowded, long. Children had run themselves empty, collapsing into sleep with that total trust only the young possess. Larry's wife had stood close to him, shoulder to shoulder, their shared smiles speaking a language made of years.

"I can drive," she said again at the car. Not insistently. Just an offering.

Larry heard what she *didn't* say: *You look tired.*

He laughed it off. Opened the door. Took the keys.

"I've got it," he said, and believed it.

The road unfurled like a promise. Dark. Familiar. Quiet enough to feel safe. The radio murmured something nostalgic. The kids slept. The world narrowed to headlights and the gentle sway of asphalt.

Larry's eyelids grew heavy.

He blinked.

Larry felt the first blink steal time.

Then another.

Then the space between them stretched too wide.

He never remembered closing his eyes.

Rolled the window down.

Cold air slapped his face, sharp enough to sting. He welcomed it, inhaled deeply, telling himself he just needed five more minutes. Just the next turn. Just the next mile.

The last thing he remembered clearly was his wife speaking his name.

Not loud.

Concerned.

Then the road *disappeared*.

Only opening them into chaos........................

The dreams did not arrive all at once.

At first they were fragments: a jolt in the gut, the sense of falling, the echo of his wife saying his name in a tone that cut deeper than fear. He woke shaking, breath ragged, the bed alien beneath him.

Weeks passed. The fragments knitted themselves together.

The crash became a ritual.

Sometimes the dream began at the event, with the folding chairs and fluorescent lights. Sometimes it began at the car, with keys heavy in his palm. Sometimes it began on the road itself, the trees leaning inward like witnesses.

The details sharpened.

The radio song changed, always to something he recognized. The hum of tires grew louder. The road bent differently each night, but always ended the same way.

Impact came without mercy.

Larry woke screaming, throat raw, hands clawing at sheets that were never a steering wheel but always felt like one. His heart battered his ribs as if trying to escape.

During the day, he functioned by imitation. He watched others speak and copied the motions. He ate because the body demanded it, though taste had abandoned him. He nodded when people spoke of healing, of time, of accidents.

At night, time did not move.

It circled.

Larry woke screaming.

Every night.

Sometimes it was the sound first—a thunderclap of metal, a noise too large to belong in the world. Sometimes it was silence so complete it rang in his ears.

Sometimes he dreamed he was still driving.

The trees leaned inward. The road narrowed. His hands slipped on the steering wheel, slick with sweat. His wife turned toward him, mouth open, eyes wide.

"Larry—"

Then everything folded.

He woke gasping, heart hammering, fingers clenched as if still gripping the wheel. The bed was always soaked with sweat. His throat burned from screaming.

He never dreamed of himself dying.

Only of surviving.

Only of crawling out.

Only of seeing the car torn open like paper, of seeing the shapes inside that no longer looked like people, of hearing himself begging for forgiveness that no one was left to hear.

He couldn't drive anymore.

He couldn't sit in the passenger seat.

He couldn't close his eyes without seeing headlights fracture and trees rush forward like accusations.

The house became unbearable.

Every room echoed with absence. Shoes by the door that would never be worn again. Toys that still held fingerprints. A couch with an empty space that screamed louder than grief.

People told him it wasn't his fault.

That fatigue happens.

That accidents happen.

Larry nodded.

He smiled.

He thanked them.

Then he went home and punished himself anyway.

Sleep became a battleground. Wakefulness wasn't better. His mind replayed the moment endlessly, stretching the seconds before impact into cruel eternities. In some versions, his wife reached the wheel. In others, the kids woke and cried. In all of them, Larry felt the moment his eyes closed.

You should have let her drive.

The thought came first as his own.

Later, it arrived with clarity.

Precision.

You knew you were tired.

Larry sat in his wrecked living room one night, surrounded by photos he hadn't yet found the strength to put away, and felt the air change.

Not colder.

Focused.

You chose pride over safety, the thought continued, gentle and devastating.

Larry pressed his palms into his eyes. "Stop," he whispered.

The thought didn't stop.

It refined.

That was how **Caligo** entered his life—not as a monster, not as a voice from the dark, but as a perfect mirror for guilt Larry already carried.

The nightmares grew more detailed.

More accurate.

Caligo slowed the crash down, forcing Larry to experience every fraction of a second. The sound of tires losing grip. The lurch of gravity. The moment when physics decided there was no escape.

Sometimes Larry dreamed he woke just before impact.

Sometimes he dreamed his wife was driving and *he* was the one who insisted she keep going.

Every variation ended the same way.

The only constant was that Larry lived.

Survival is the punishment, Caligo observed.

Larry stopped eating. Stopped answering calls. He began sitting in his car at night, hands resting on the steering wheel, engine off, staring at the dark road ahead.

"I just want it to stop," he said once, aloud.

The presence leaned closer.

You know how.

The dreams began to *correct themselves.*

If Larry tried to wake before the crash, the dream adjusted—his eyes opened sooner, the road narrowing, the danger clearer. If he tried to slow down, the brakes softened, spongy and unresponsive. If he tried to hand the wheel to his wife, his hands refused to let go.

The dreams wanted something from him.

One night, as the impact loomed, a thought arrived with terrifying clarity:

You chose this.

Larry woke sobbing, nails bitten to the quick.

"No," he whispered to the empty room.

The room did not answer.

The next night, the thought returned, refined:

You were warned.

The night after that:

You were asked.

Larry stopped sleeping.

He paced the house until dawn, touching objects that anchored him to the present. Shoes by the door. A jacket on the hook. The couch where his wife used to sit, legs tucked beneath her, pretending to be annoyed when he took too long choosing a movie.

Memory became a weapon he wielded against himself.

And then, quietly, something else joined the memories.

It didn't announce itself.

It didn't look like a monster.

It felt like *focus.*

The dreams slowed further, time stretching until seconds felt like hours. Larry could see the grain of the dashboard, the dust in the air, the reflection of his own eyes in the windshield.

A presence watched with him.

You see now, it thought, and the thought fit perfectly into the groove guilt had already carved.

Larry tried to pray.

The words fell apart in his mouth.

Forgiveness, the presence seemed to test, tasting the word like something foreign. *Explain it.*

Larry couldn't.

He only knew the weight in his chest grew heavier when he tried.

The presence grew patient.

Night after night, it replayed the moment—not to punish him, but to *perfect* it. Each iteration removed excuses, softened edges, stripped away randomness until only choice remained.

You could have stopped, it insisted.

Larry believed it.

He began sitting in his car long after midnight, engine off, keys resting in his palm. The driver's seat became a confession booth. He stared through the windshield at the empty road, feeling watched, accompanied.

"I just want it to stop," he said once, aloud.

The presence leaned closer, pleased.

It can.

That was when Larry finally understood the name whispered through his thoughts—not spoken, but *known*.

Caligo

Invite me in, Larry was drained at this point and his only thought was if Caligo could ease this pain.

So Larry replied, OK.

Caligo swiftly took the seat in Larry's mind. Lets go for a drive Caligo stated.

Larry was in the driver seat no sure of how he even got there.

The final drive felt eerily calm.

Larry's hands were steady. His breathing even. The road accepted him without resistance, empty and wide, the night offering no witnesses.

As speed built, the world narrowed again—but this time, there was no panic.

The speed felt different once it passed a certain point.

The car stopped responding like a machine and began responding like a creature—eager, unstable, hungry. The engine screamed, a pitch too high to be healthy, vibrating through Larry's bones until his teeth buzzed. The headlights tunneled forward, carving a pale corridor through the dark, the edges of the world blurring into a smear of black and green.

The steering wheel shuddered.

Not violently—just enough.

Larry felt the first tug, the subtle sideways pull that told him physics was beginning to make decisions without him. His hands tightened automatically, muscles reacting before thought could catch up.

The road bent.

The bend came too quickly.

The tires protested, a shrill, panicked sound that cut through the engine's roar. The car drifted—not a skid, not yet—just a soft, terrible refusal to obey. The headlights swung wide, illuminating trees that were suddenly much closer than they should have been.

Larry's stomach dropped.

Time fractured.

In the space between heartbeats, his mind flooded with images. He felt as if his family was in the car with him, his daughter's hair fanned across his shoulder, his son's sleepy humming, his wife's hand warm and trusting. The weight of them pressed into him, heavier than gravity.

He tried to turn.

The wheel resisted, stiff and wrong, jerking in his grip as if something else had seized it from the other side. The road vanished entirely, replaced by bark and shadow and the blinding white flare of reflected light.

The impact did not feel like a single moment.

It felt like *layers*.

First came sound—an impossible explosion that swallowed everything else, a concussive roar that seemed to tear the night apart. Then came force, a crushing, all-encompassing pressure that folded metal inward with violent certainty.

Larry's body was thrown forward, then sideways, then nowhere at all.

The world inverted.

Glass burst outward in a spray of sharp, glittering fragments that caught the headlights for a fraction of a second before disappearing into darkness. The windshield collapsed inward, the dashboard surged up, the steering wheel lurched violently against his chest.

The car screamed as it died.

The trees did not move.

Everything that could bend, bent.

Everything that could break, did.

Larry's thoughts scattered, stripped of language, reduced to sensation—pressure, heat, the taste of blood where his teeth cut his tongue, the crushing weight pinning him where the driver's seat used to be.

The engine coughed once.

Then went silent.

In the sudden quiet, smaller sounds emerged: the ticking of cooling metal, the hiss of escaping fluids, the faint crackle of something electrical failing.

Larry tried to breathe.

The air came in wrong—shallow, sharp, burning. Each breath scraped through his chest like broken glass, sending pain radiating outward in blinding waves. His vision pulsed, narrowing to a tunnel that flickered at the edges.

He couldn't feel his legs.

He couldn't move his arms.

The steering wheel pressed into him at an unnatural angle, trapping him in a posture that made no sense. His head lolled to the side, cheek pressed against something cold and wet.

He thought of the road.

Of how empty it had been.

Of how certain he had felt.

The certainty shattered.

In the final moments, as the dark crept inward, a presence settled over him—not comforting, not cruel, simply *observant.*

This is where it ends, it seemed to say, not with satisfaction, but with completion.

Larry's vision dimmed completely.

The night closed.

Later—much later—others would find the wreck twisted around the tree, the front end collapsed into itself, the driver's side unrecognizable. They would speak in careful voices, using words like *instant* and *nothing could be done.*

But the road would remember.

The air would hold the echo of speed abruptly stolen.

And somewhere, far from the wreckage, **Caligo** would withdraw from the ruin it had no longer any use for—confused by the faint, unfamiliar residue left behind.

Not guilt.

But something loosening.

Something like release.....................

Months later, Mara stood near a roadside memorial, the air thick with a sensation she could not name. She felt the *pause* in the world, the sense of a decision still being made again and again.

Mara heard Larry.

Not his name.

His *pause.*

She felt it standing near the roadside memorial months afterward—the inexplicable heaviness, the sense of a decision endlessly replayed. The echo of a man who had survived the wrong thing for too long.

She closed her eyes.

She pressed a hand to her chest.

"You don't have to keep driving,"

"This isn't yours to keep," she whispered, though she didn't know who she spoke to.

But somewhere far away, in a darkness that no longer fed it, Caligo recoiled—angry, confused, starved by something it could not understand.

Forgiveness.

Larry's echo softened.

The road breathed again.

But Caligo remained.

Waiting.

CHAPTER TWENTY

CALIGO LEARNS

Mara had begun to notice patterns, but seeing them in sequence was something else entirely. The echoes of those it had touched—the first, the second, the third—stacked themselves in her mind like layers of a dark, stained manuscript.

Sara had been subtle. Caligo entered her slowly, like a whisper curling around the edges of consciousness. It never shouted. It didn't rush. It magnified every guilt-laden thought until surrender seemed like the only way to stop the relentless looping. With her, it worked through repetition and weariness, leaving traces in empty rooms, echoes in the quiet. Her death was quiet, almost serene in its inevitability—a final relinquishing of control, a body giving way to the relentless gravity of grief, leaving the house heavy with absence.

Mark had been different. Caligo had discovered in him a sharper, more volatile edge. It didn't merely amplify memory—it toyed with it. It showed him vivid replay after vivid replay, dragging him deeper into the horror of the past he could not change: his children burning before his eyes, screams tearing through his chest. Caligo teased the mind, stretching seconds into unbearable eternities, amplifying helplessness to a point that made surrender feel like a small mercy. When Mark finally gave in, it had forced him not into a quiet dissolution, but into an active, horrifying final act—the body a stage for the consequences of the mind's collapse.

Larry's crash revealed yet another layer. Here, Caligo had refined patience and escalation. It did not rely on whispered guilt alone. It did not simply magnify memory. Larry's exhaustion, his pride, his insistence on control—it all became a crucible. The road itself was a weapon. Each blink, each lapse of consciousness was a step deeper into terror. Caligo allowed the night to stretch, distorted time to fracture reality, manipulated physicality through perception, and let anticipation become unbearable. Unlike Sara, whose surrender was internal, and Mark, whose surrender was in vivid repetition, Larry's surrender was enacted in the world—but orchestrated entirely in his mind until the very last second. Every car, every curve, every shadow along the roadside became a tool of the entity, a test of how far it could push before the inevitable release.

Mara could feel the difference. The echoes of Sara hovered in her apartment like soft, muted warnings—gentle tremors of sorrow she could acknowledge and let go. Mark's echoes thrashed violently in the corners of her mind, screams that demanded attention, making her flinch, making her remember the magnitude of trauma. Larry's echo was more subtle at first, a pulse in the air, a hesitation in the roadside wind, a weight pressing into memory. But it was sharp in a different way—it carried the tension of a man who had fought, resisted, and ultimately been perfected by the method. Caligo had learned to twist the threads of circumstance itself, to exploit pride and fatigue, to shape the environment into a labyrinth of inevitable doom.

It was not just about guilt anymore. It was about **precision**. About finding the exact combination of memory, pride, exhaustion, and circumstance that would ensure surrender. Where it had once whispered, it now orchestrated. Where it had once magnified, it now conducted. And Mara understood, with a chill that settled in her chest, that every echo left behind—Sara, Mark, Larry—was a rehearsal, a test, a refinement of its patience and cruelty.

Caligo was learning.

And if it had a next victim, it would be unlike anything before.

Mara began mapping them in her mind.

Sara: quiet, internal surrender, left traces in spaces.

Mark: raw, visceral, screamed in memory, demanded attention.

Larry: precise, environmental, shaped the world around him into a trap.

She could see it now. Caligo was **learning**. Each victim refined its approach: the whispering patience with Sara, the obsessive replay with Mark, the orchestration with Larry. Each death was a lesson. Each echo a test.

It was Mara's turn to understand the pattern.

The first sign was subtle—a hesitation in her own thoughts, a fleeting sensation of déjà vu while walking past an empty street corner. She felt the soft pressure of observation, like breath on her neck when no one was behind her. Then came the fragments: a child's laugh that didn't exist, a knock at a door she hadn't opened, a glint of reflection in a car window that didn't belong to any living being.

And then the echoes began to speak to each other.

Sara's sorrow brushed against Mark's terror. Larry's tension pressed into them both. Mara could feel them layered on top of each other, a chorus of loss, guilt, and inevitability. It was as if the victims themselves were trapped in a rehearsal of their final moments, and she was watching from just outside the frame.

Her chest tightened. She understood the cruel elegance of Caligo's design. It never forced entry. It never created guilt where there was none. It took what existed, amplified it, and waited. When it was resisted, it grew angry. When ignored, it waited longer. With each victim, it learned a little more: how long a mind could endure, how precise an environment could be manipulated, how subtle a whisper could push someone toward surrender.

Mara shivered.

If Caligo was learning from each death, then she had a chance—and a warning. She had seen what it could do. She had felt it in the echoes. Sara's quiet despair. Mark's screaming helplessness. Larry's orchestrated inevitability.

And now it was whispering to her.

Not in words, not yet. She didn't feel it pressing. She felt it **testing**, like a shadow brushing against the edges of her mind, seeing what she carried. Mara held her breath and waited.

For hours, it circled, patient. She remembered the lessons. She remembered her own failures, her own grief—but unlike the others, she understood that she **could not give it permission**. That was its weakness. That was its only limit.

And the echoes—Sara, Mark, Larry—shifted around her. Not angry. Not pleading. Just waiting. Watching. Teaching.

The crescendo of understanding came in a single thought, crystal clear: **Caligo could not take what it could not be invited to hold.**

It had been perfecting itself, learning precision, learning patience, learning cruelty—but it could not breach her without her consent.

And Mara realized: the echoes, the lessons, the refinements, were not just terror—they were **a map**.

Sara taught patience—how to wait, how guilt festers quietly.

Mark taught escalation—how terror can spiral, uncontained, if the mind does not resist.

Larry taught precision—how circumstance itself could be weaponized, how reality bends when attention wavers.

The map showed the path, and Mara was determined not to follow it.

Caligo waited.

The darkness outside her windows pulsed with quiet patience, hungry for the moment she might falter. But Mara had already begun the countermeasure—not force, not resistance, but **acknowledgment, understanding, and preparation**. She would not ignore the echoes, but she would not let them drag her into surrender.

Somewhere deep in the shadows, Caligo twitched with anger. It could sense her clarity. It could feel that its lessons, its refinements, its cruel orchestration, were failing before it could use them. The echoes—Sara, Mark, Larry—remained in the quiet spaces, their weight still pressing at the edges of the world. And Mara understood that she was standing on the knife-edge between surrender and mastery, between victimhood and survival.

And for the first time, she felt a plan form in the silence: a way not just to survive, but to **stop the cycle**.

Caligo had learned from its victims—but Mara would learn from Caligo.

And she would be ready.

CHAPTER TWENTY ONE

THE MINUTE THAT NEVER ENDED (MARA'S PAIN)

The bathroom is warm.

That is always the first thing Mara notices.

Steam softens the edges of the room, clinging to the mirror until her reflection blurs into a pale shape she barely recognizes. The overhead light hums faintly, steady and ordinary. The tub is half-full, water glassy and still, reflecting the ceiling like a second world beneath the first.

Her child sits in the bath.

Alive.

Laughing.

Small hands slap the surface, sending water over the rim in careless splashes that dot the tile floor. The sound is bright and harmless, the sound of something that is supposed to be safe. Mara smiles, her chest loosening despite the tightness she always carries now.

This is the part that hurts the most.

Because nothing is wrong yet.

She reaches for the towel—blue, folded neatly on the counter. She remembers thinking she should move it closer. She remembers noticing how warm the room felt, how pink her child's cheeks were from the bath.

The phone rings.

The sound cuts through the room sharply, wrong in its urgency. Mara flinches even now, even though she knows what comes next. Her heart stutters, dread blooming before her mind has caught up.

"It's okay," she says automatically, smiling down into the tub. "Mommy will be right back."

She steps into the hallway.

The phone rings again.

She answers.

That's it.

That's the moment that never ends.

The memory stretches here, pulling apart the seconds until they feel thick and resistant. The voice on the other end of the line is unimportant—mundane, even—but every word takes time. Every pause grows teeth.

Mara's fingers curl around the phone, knuckles whitening.

She feels it then—the shift. The sense that something has gone wrong behind her, just out of sight. Her chest tightens. Her breath shortens.

She hangs up.

The hallway feels too long.

When she reaches the bathroom, the air is still warm, but the room is wrong.

The water is too calm.

Her child's head tilts at an angle that makes no sense. Hair fans out across the surface, drifting gently. The mouth is just below the waterline.

Mara screams.

She drops to her knees, water soaking her clothes as she plunges her arms into the tub, lifting her child with frantic strength. The weight is wrong—too heavy, too slack. Skin is cool in places it should still be warm.

"No," she sobs. "No, no, no—"

She presses her mouth to her child's, breath coming in ragged bursts she can't control. Her hands shake violently as she tries to remember what to do, tries to make her body move faster than terror allows.

Nothing happens.

The world collapses inward.

She doesn't remember dialing the phone again. She doesn't remember screaming into it. She remembers only the waiting—and the way time seemed to stop moving forward at all.

CHAPTER TWENTY-TWO

CHAPTER TWENTY TWO

WHAT SHE DIDN'T HEAR

The silence is what stays.

Not the water. Not the bathroom.

The silence afterward.

Mara remembers the way the house seemed to pull away from her, as if embarrassed by what had happened inside it. Sounds came from far away, muffled, distorted. Her own breathing felt unreal, like it belonged to someone else.

She carried her child into the living room.

The weight felt unbearable in her arms, wrong in a way that had nothing to do with size. She kept thinking—this isn't how it's supposed to feel. This isn't how this is supposed to go.

The memory fractures here.

Replays.

Sometimes the sirens arrive quickly. Sometimes they take too long. Sometimes she's alone for so long she begins to doubt anyone is coming at all. Mara visualized her daughter drowning in the tub. The details shift just enough to leave space for questions.

Did she cry when she left?

Did she reach for the edge of the tub?

Did she slip under quietly, or did she fight?

Mara never knows.

That uncertainty gnaws at her more viciously than certainty ever could.

If I hadn't answered the phone—

The thought loops endlessly, cutting deeper each time it returns. The memory resets to the beginning again and again, relentless in its precision.

Back to the warmth.

Back to laughter.

Back to the ringing.

Each time, Mara tries something different.

She ignores the phone.

It keeps ringing.

She tells herself she'll wait.

The sound grows louder.

She rushes back sooner.

She's still too late.

Eventually, she stops trying.

She collapses onto the bathroom floor as the memory plays out without her participation. The water overflows. The phone rings. The silence follows.

Mara rocks back and forth, hands pressed to her face, breathing hard. Her thoughts feel worn thin, frayed by repetition.

"You didn't mean to," she whispers to the empty room. "I know I didn't mean to."

The words don't help.

They never do.

The guilt doesn't lessen. It sharpens. It reshapes itself around new questions, new imagined seconds she can never recover.

Somewhere in the endless replay, Mara realizes something that terrifies her more than the memory itself:

She can no longer remember her child growing up.

Not clearly.

The memory of the bath has swallowed everything else—the laughter, the milestones, the small ordinary moments that once filled her days.

There is only the tub now.

Only the ringing phone.

Only the minute she walked away.

Mara presses her palms into the tile, grounding herself in the cold, breathing through the ache in her chest. She doesn't know how long she stays there.

She only knows the memory never truly ends.

It waits.

And it always begins again the moment she lets her guard down.

CHAPTER TWENTY THREE

WHEN SILENCE LEANS BACK

M ara knew she was no longer alone the moment the quiet responded.

She was sitting on the bathroom floor, back against the tub, knees pulled tight to her chest. The room had finished resetting itself—the warmth restored, the mirror fogged just enough to blur her face, the light steady again. The memory waited, poised to begin once more.

But it didn't.

The phone did not ring.

Her child did not laugh.

The stillness stretched, elastic and unnatural, until Mara felt it pressing against her ribs from the inside. She held her breath without realizing it, afraid that even breathing might trigger the loop.

"Okay," she whispered to the room. "Okay. I know something's wrong."

The silence shifted.

Not broke—*shifted*. As if it had weight, and that weight had decided to settle somewhere else. The air behind her cooled, carrying with it the faintest suggestion of depth, like standing at the edge of a long, lightless hallway.

Mara did not turn around.

She didn't need to.

"You changed it," she said, voice trembling despite her effort to steady it. "You changed the memory."

There was no answer.

Instead, a sensation brushed the edge of her thoughts—not a touch, not a sound, but a *recognition*. The unsettling awareness of being seen in a way that had nothing to do with eyes.

Her stomach clenched. "You're not welcome here."

The response came slowly, unfolding inside her mind like a careful thought she might have had herself.

I'm already where you look.

Mara's breath hitched. The voice—if it could be called that—was calm, unhurried, and disturbingly familiar. It carried her cadence, her pauses, her restraint. It didn't intrude. It *rested*.

She pushed herself upright, palms sliding against the tile. "You're the one who leaves things behind," she said. "The echoes. The children I hear. You did that."

The presence did not deny it.

It seemed to consider her instead.

You hear what remains, it replied.

Most people don't.

Anger flared hot and sudden, cutting through her fear. "They're not yours," Mara snapped. "You don't get to—"

I never take what isn't offered.

The words were not defensive. They were factual.

Mara stood on shaking legs. The bathroom felt subtly larger now, its corners receding just enough to make distance feel unreliable. The mirror reflected her alone—but the space around her reflection seemed... deeper than it should have been.

"You've been circling me," she said. "You didn't touch me before. You waited."

You were busy listening, the voice answered.

Grief makes excellent doors.

Mara's hands curled into fists. "I didn't invite you."

The pressure in the room eased slightly—not retreating, but acknowledging the statement, like a nod.

No, it agreed.

You didn't.

The admission unsettled her more than denial would have. "Then why now?"

For the first time, the presence felt... strained.

Not angry.

Focused.

Because your memory is changing, it said.

And it isn't supposed to.

Mara's heart began to race. "You don't control it."

A pause.

Then, faint irritation—subtle as a temperature drop.

I observe patterns, the voice replied.

I don't alter them.

"Liar."

You are reliving the minute you walked away, it continued, ignoring the accusation.

You have done so faithfully for years. But now you are noticing what you didn't before.

Mara swallowed hard. Images pressed at the edges of her thoughts—the grip of small fingers on porcelain, the word *Mama* spoken clearly, fearfully.

"That didn't happen," she whispered.

You don't know that.

Her knees nearly gave out. "Don't," she said. "You don't get to tell me what I remember."

The presence leaned closer—not spatially, but *intentionally.* The pressure behind her eyes returned, heavier now, testing.

I don't create guilt, it said.

I only give it room.

Mara shook her head, backing away until her shoulder blades hit the door. "I forgave myself," she said, though the words sounded thin even to her own ears. "I've tried."

The silence thickened.

Something in it hardened.

Forgiveness landed strangely in the space between them—like a concept introduced into a language that didn't have a word for it.

You say that, the voice replied carefully.

Yet you return. Again and again.

"That doesn't mean—"

It means the door is still there.

Mara's chest burned. Tears blurred her vision. "I miss my child," she said. "That's not guilt. That's love."

The presence recoiled.

Just slightly.

Not in pain—but in confusion.

Love did not fit its structure. Love did not loop cleanly. Love did not sharpen the way guilt did. It spread outward instead, softening edges, making memories uneven and difficult to hold.

For the first time, Mara felt something like leverage.

"You don't understand that part," she said softly. "Do you?"

The room cooled further.

You're very close to exhaustion, the voice said, the calm thinning. *Most people don't last this long.*

Mara wiped her face with the heel of her hand. "I'm not most people."

The presence grew taut, irritation bleeding through its restraint. Not rage—yet—but a brittle tension, like ice under pressure.

You don't have to keep hurting, it offered.
You don't have to keep listening.

Mara laughed weakly. "That's the first honest thing you've said."

The silence leaned in again, waiting.

Waiting for the moment she would ask how.

Waiting for the invitation it could not take without permission.

Mara closed her eyes, breathing through the ache in her chest, through the memory that waited just beyond the door of the moment.

"I know who you are now," she said. "And you're not getting in."

The presence did not leave.

It did not advance.

It simply remained—angry at her resistance, unsettled by her forgiveness, anchored by her attention.

In the quiet space between them, **Caligo** waited.

And for the first time since her child died, Mara understood that survival did not mean silence.

It meant choosing which voices were allowed to stay.

CHAPTER TWENTY FOUR

WHAT FEEDS ON ATTENTION

Mara did not sleep.

She learned quickly that sleep was where **Caligo** was most articulate.

So she stayed awake, lights on, television murmuring without meaning, coffee cooling untouched in her hands. She let exhaustion scrape her raw, because raw was better than open. Raw still had edges.

It was during the third night—when time began to lose its sequence—that she realized Caligo was not *following* her.

It was *studying* her.

Not in the way a predator watches prey, but in the way a mathematician stares at a problem that refuses to resolve. Patient. Precise. Increasingly irritated by inconsistency.

The echoes of children still came sometimes. Faint. Displaced. Not memories—residue. She understood now they were not hauntings. They were afterimages. Places where Caligo had once been invited and then left behind something it didn't know how to retrieve.

She wrote everything down.

Patterns mattered.

Caligo never spoke when she was angry.

It never spoke when she cried.

It spoke when she *focused*.

When she replayed the memory deliberately. When she followed the thread of guilt instead of cutting it short. When she examined the moment she walked away like it might finally confess something new.

Attention was the key.

Caligo didn't push. It didn't coerce. It didn't whisper temptations or offer comfort. It waited for a mind already turning inward, already looping, already punishing itself.

Then it stepped into the rhythm.

Mara tested it.

The next time the bathroom memory began, she did not resist. She stood in the doorway and let the warmth settle, let the hum of the light exist without flinching.

Her child laughed.

The phone rang.

Mara closed her eyes—and instead of following the panic, she did something new.

She spoke.

"I forgive myself."

The words were clumsy. Unpracticed. They felt false in her mouth, like a language she had never been allowed to learn.

The room reacted immediately.

The light flickered hard—once, twice. The temperature dropped sharply, steam collapsing off the mirror in rivulets. The pressure behind her eyes surged, not painful but *tense*, like something bracing.

That doesn't belong here, Caligo said.

Mara opened her eyes. "Why not?"

Silence stretched, brittle now.

Because it ends the sequence.

Understanding settled into her chest with a quiet, devastating clarity.

Caligo did not feed on pain.

It fed on *continuation*.

Guilt that resolved was useless. Grief that softened lost its edges. Forgiveness—true forgiveness, the kind that did not deny the harm but released the endless self-trial—collapsed the loop entirely.

"You can't follow me there," Mara said.

The presence pressed closer, agitation radiating through the air like static.

You're lying to yourself.

"No," she replied. "I'm choosing something you can't process."

The memory stuttered. The phone rang too early. Her child's laugh cut off mid-breath. The room struggled to maintain its shape.

Caligo grew sharper.

Not louder—but more *narrow*.

You left, it said.

That is fact.

"Yes."

You could have stayed.

"Yes."

And because you didn't—

"I forgive myself anyway."

The words landed like a fracture.

The bathroom collapsed.

Mara found herself back in her living room, heart racing, breath ragged. The echoes were gone. The air felt... empty. Not peaceful. Not safe. But *cleared*, like ground after a fire.

Caligo did not speak again that night.

When it returned, it did so differently.

Not in memories—but in irritation.

Lights dimmed when she ignored her thoughts. Sounds sharpened when she focused on the present. The presence lurked at the edges of her awareness, restless, pacing without feet.

She realized then that ignoring Caligo was worse than resisting it.

Resistance still acknowledged it.

Ignoring it starved it.

So she stopped engaging.

When the memory began, she let it pass without entering. When guilt rose, she named it and set it aside. When her mind circled the what-ifs, she grounded herself in what *was*.

Each time, the presence grew more unstable.

You're breaking the pattern, Caligo accused one evening, its composure thinning.

"That's the point."

You don't understand what you're risking.

Mara almost laughed. "You don't understand forgiveness."

A long pause followed.

Longer than any before.

Explain it.

The request was not curious.

It was desperate.

Mara closed her eyes, choosing her words carefully. "Forgiveness doesn't erase what happened. It just means I stop using it as a weapon against myself."

The silence that followed was... wrong.

Dense. Pressurized.

Caligo recoiled—not physically, but conceptually. The idea did not fit within it. There was no mechanism for mercy without admission. No structure for acceptance without surrender.

Then nothing remains, it said.

"Exactly."

The presence flared—anger at last, sharp and cold. The room darkened as if shadows had learned how to lean inward.

If there is no guilt, Caligo said, *there is no door.*

Mara's hands trembled, but she held her ground. "Then you should leave."

The anger sharpened further—not explosive, but *focused*. A blade without a handle.

You still hear them, it said, grasping.
The echoes.

"Yes," Mara answered softly. "And I'll carry them. Not for you. For me."

The pressure snapped.

The room lightened. The air loosened.

Caligo did not vanish—but it withdrew, shrinking back into the places where her attention no longer lingered. Furious. Incomplete. Unable to follow her where the loop no longer closed.

Mara sank into a chair, exhausted beyond measure, tears finally coming—not of guilt, but of release.

She understood now.

Caligo was not a monster of claws or fangs.

It was a function.

A parasite of unresolved moments.

And for the first time since her child died, Mara knew exactly how to starve it.

By living forward.

By forgiving without permission.

By refusing to listen.

CHAPTER TWENTY-FIVE

CHAPTER TWENTY FIVE

THE LAST DOOR

M ara understood, at last, that the battle would not look like a battle at all.

There would be no running, no screaming, no desperate bargains whispered into the dark. **Caligo** did not fear confrontation.

It feared *resolution*.

The realization settled into her bones as she stood in the center of her apartment, lights off, windows open to the night. She had stripped the space of distractions—no television, no music, no noise to fracture her attention. If Caligo fed on focus, then she would decide *what* deserved it.

The air thickened almost immediately.

Not cold. Not hot. Simply *dense*, as though the room were slowly filling with unseen water. Shadows stretched longer than their sources. Corners deepened. The familiar pressure bloomed behind her eyes, heavier than it had ever been.

You're inviting collapse, Caligo observed, its voice taut with irritation.

Mara exhaled slowly. "No. I'm closing the loop."

The presence swelled, offended by the calm in her tone.

The memory surged forward without warning.

The bathroom.

Steam. Light. The tub.

Her child.

This time, Caligo did not ease her into it. It threw her into the moment with force, saturating every detail—the echo of laughter, the slick tile beneath her feet, the ring of the phone slicing through the air like a blade.

Mistakes demand consequence, Caligo said, pressing down. *Attention sustains truth.*

Mara staggered but did not fall.

She had lived this moment in pieces for years. Caligo had sharpened it, slowed it, rearranged it. But now she saw the shape beneath the cruelty.

"You need me to keep asking *what if,*" she said, voice trembling but steady. "You need me to believe there was a version where no one died."

The phone rang again—too loud, too close.

There was, Caligo hissed. *You just didn't choose it.*

Mara's heart slammed against her ribs. Tears burned her eyes—but she stayed.

"No," she said. "There was a version where I answered the phone. And a version where I didn't. And in every version, I was human."

The memory shuddered.

Water sloshed violently in the tub, rising too high, spilling over the edge. The child's laughter warped, stretching into something panicked, overlapping with itself.

Caligo leaned in, furious now.

You left, it repeated.

You left.

"Yes," Mara said, stepping closer to the tub. "And I will carry that. But I will not let you turn it into a weapon."

The pressure became unbearable.

The walls bowed inward. The light flickered violently. The phone rang without pause, its sound drilling into her skull. The presence clawed for her focus, for her shame, for the place she had always opened without realizing it.

Say it, Caligo demanded.

Say you failed.

Mara closed her eyes.

And for the first time, she did not brace for the pain.

"I did everything I could with the person I was in that moment," she said softly. "And I forgive her."

The words were not loud.

They did not shake the room.

They did something worse.

They *ended* something.

The phone went silent.

The water froze mid-surge, suspended unnaturally before collapsing back into the tub. The laughter cut off—not into screams, not into echoes—just *gone.*

Caligo recoiled.

The presence shrank sharply, its composure cracking.

You're erasing yourself, it said, anger flaring cold and sharp.

Without guilt, you are nothing.

Mara opened her eyes.

"I'm everything," she replied. "I'm the one who loved them."

The memory began to dissolve—not burning, not tearing, but *fading*, like fog under morning light. The bathroom peeled away, tile by tile, sound by sound, until only darkness remained.

Caligo surged forward, no longer patient, no longer controlled. The air screamed as pressure spiked, shadows twisting into impossible depth.

You still hear them, it lashed out.

You still feel them.

"Yes," Mara said, tears streaming freely now. "And that's not yours."

The echoes of children—the distant voices she had carried for so long—rose gently around her. Not screaming. Not pleading.

Remembering.

Caligo writhed within the space of her mind, furious, disoriented.

They bind you, it snarled.

"They remind me why I survived."

The darkness began to recede.

Not violently—but *inevitably.*

Caligo strained against it, pulling inward, compressing itself into tighter and tighter focus, desperate for a fracture, a hesitation, a single unclosed wound.

You need me, it said, its voice thinning.

Without pain, you forget.

Mara knelt in the empty dark, pressing her hand to her chest. "No," she whispered. "Without you, I remember *everything*—not just the worst part."

The last door closed.

There was no scream.

No explosion.

Caligo collapsed inward, folding into itself like a shadow deprived of light, dragged backward into the spaces where attention could no longer reach it. Furious. Starving. Incomplete.

Then—

Nothing.

The pressure lifted.

The darkness softened.

Mara was alone.

She remained there for a long time, breathing, crying, feeling the weight of grief without the blade of guilt attached to it. It hurt—but it no longer consumed.

When she finally stood, the apartment felt different. Not safe. Not healed.

But *hers*.

She knew Caligo was not destroyed.

Things like that were never destroyed.

They were forgotten.

And forgiveness—true forgiveness—was the deepest darkness it would ever know.

CHAPTER TWENTY SIX

THE WEIGHT THAT IS GONE

H ealing did not arrive all at once.

It came quietly, in ordinary moments that Mara did not recognize as victories until much later.

Morning light through clean windows.

Coffee that stayed warm long enough to finish.

Silence that did not lean back.

Mara woke without panic for the first time in years and lay still, waiting for the familiar pressure behind her eyes—the tightening, the expectation of pain, the reflexive reach for guilt.

It never came.

Her chest rose and fell easily. The room was just a room. No corners deepened. No memories pressed forward demanding replay. Her mind felt... spacious. Not empty. Spacious.

She cried then—not because she was hurting, but because she wasn't.

The bathroom door stood open.

She walked past it without stopping.

That alone felt like a miracle.

Days unfolded gently. Mara returned to routines she had once abandoned—grocery shopping without dissociating in the aisles, showers without bracing herself against the tile, phone calls without dread coiling in her stomach. She let herself linger in moments instead of rushing through them as if time itself were dangerous.

The memories still existed.

They always would.

But they were *whole* now.

She could remember her child's laugh without the sound collapsing into water. She could remember bath time without the moment freezing at the threshold of disaster. The memory no longer narrowed to the worst second—it expanded, softened, regained context.

Love returned first.

Guilt did not follow.

Mara began speaking about her child again. Not in hushed tones. Not with apologies layered into every sentence. She told stories—real ones. Funny ones. Ordinary ones. Stories that reminded her that her child had *lived*, not just died.

And each time she did, the space inside her chest widened instead of closing.

That was how she knew it was real.

Forgiveness did not erase responsibility.

It released punishment.

She visited the park again—the one she had avoided for years because the sight of children once felt like knives. She sat on a bench and watched parents chase toddlers, watched laughter spill freely into the open air.

It hurt.

But it did not hollow her out.

She pressed a hand to her heart and breathed through it. "I loved you," she whispered—not to the absence, but to the memory itself.

And for the first time, the words did not echo back accusingly.

They simply stayed.

Mara began volunteering at a local grief support group—not as a guide, not as someone healed beyond pain, but as someone who understood the difference between remembering and punishing oneself. She listened more than she spoke. When she did speak, she chose her words carefully.

"I don't think forgiveness is forgetting," she told a woman whose hands shook like Mara's once had. "I think it's choosing not to keep reopening the wound."

She meant every word.

At night, Mara slept deeply.

Dreams came, but they were no longer traps. Her child appeared sometimes—whole, laughing, alive within the logic of dreams that did not demand realism. Mara woke from those dreams with tears on her cheeks and peace in her bones.

No pressure followed.

No presence waited.

She had starved it completely.

Or so it seemed.

Far below her awareness—beneath thought, beneath memory, beneath the places forgiveness could reach—something remained.

Not watching.

Waiting.

In the places where light could not enter because light was no longer sought, **Caligo** existed as compression rather than form. A knot of unresolved fury. A function without fuel.

It could not move.

It could not reach.

It could not whisper.

Forgiveness had sealed the door from Mara's side—and Caligo, bound by its own nature, could not force what was not offered.

The darkness around it was absolute.

Not comforting.

Not nourishing.

Starving.

Caligo did not understand forgiveness.

It never had.

The concept remained fractured within it—an error it could not reconcile. Guilt made sense. Shame made sense. Repetition made sense.

Release did not.

And so it waited—angry, compressed, conscious in a way that bordered on pain. It could feel Mara living forward, could feel the distance growing, widening into something unreachable.

The echoes were gone.

The doors were closed.

But Caligo knew one thing with perfect clarity.

It could not leave her.

Not yet.

It could not move to another host unless Mara opened herself again—unless she invited it back in, unless she turned forgiveness inward into silence and chose annihilation over endurance.

Until then, Caligo remained in the dark.

Hungry.

Furious.

Listening for the smallest crack in healing—
the faintest hesitation—
the briefest moment where grief might mistake itself for guilt again.

Because patience was still a form of attention.

And darkness had always been very good at waiting.

CHAPTER TWENTY SEVEN

THE WAITING DARK

C aligo sat in the shadows.

Not on the street. Not in a room. Not in the corners of any building Mara walked past. It existed in the places between—the cracks of perception, the spaces where guilt had once thrived, the thin thread between consciousness and memory. For the first time, it felt *trapped*.

It had been so close.

Mara had trembled under its whispers. She had faltered at the edges of fear. But when it came to the final step—when she could have surrendered, could have invited him inside—she had not.

She had forgiven herself.

That single act shattered everything. Caligo could not enter. Could not possess. Could not unleash itself fully. It could feel Mara's mind now as a fortress—closed, resolute, impenetrable. Its patience, honed over centuries of feeding on guilt, had failed.

The darkness around it pulsed with fury.

Caligo moved, testing the bounds of its prison. The shadows were thick, pliable, but finite. It could twist them, fold them, whisper through them—but it could not leave. Not yet. Mara had built walls it could not breach. It seethed. Anger, frustration, hunger—emotions it had learned to wield against others—turned inward, coiling like a storm in a cage.

It began to plan.

First, it would wait. Patience had been its greatest weapon. Time was its ally. Mara had defeated it in the moment, but time was infinite. It could not leave, but it could *observe*. It could whisper faintly into the edges of the world, planting seeds, nudging events. It could learn again. Adapt again. Find another vulnerability. Another thread to pull.

It would not forget.

Caligo replayed the lessons of its victims in its mind. Evan, Emma, Sara, Mark, Larry—each had taught it something new about human weakness. And now, Mara had taught it something far more dangerous: humans could choose. Humans could *forgive themselves*. And when that happened, Caligo's hunger became impotent. Its method—the delicate architecture of amplification, patience, and invitation—failed.

Failure was unfamiliar.

The shadows around it thickened as if the darkness itself were aware, pressing in to contain its rage. It hissed softly—a sound more felt than heard—a promise and a warning, a whisper to the world beyond the veil.

I will find another way.

Caligo's mind stretched outward, probing, testing, skimming over the edges of perception. Every human thought, every echo of fear it could touch, became a potential map, a potential escape route. It would not strike Mara—not yet. Not until the moment was perfect. Until the world offered her an opening, a lapse in clarity, a single fraction of doubt.

And when that happened...

It would return.

The shadows swirled like smoke, coiling tighter, a storm contained but ready to burst. The air above empty streets, quiet rooms, and dark forests seemed to carry a faint tremor, a prelude to what would come. Mara had won the battle, but Caligo had not lost the war.

Somewhere far away, it waited. And it was angry.

It had learned patience before. It would learn again.

It would wait for the perfect moment. And when it struck...

The world would remember its hunger.

The darkness pulsed, hungry, patient, aware.

And the first threads of its plan had already begun.

This is not the end.

Caligo lingered in the darkness.

It began to study again.

Not the living, not yet. It studied the environment, the ways humans falter, the openings that might someday appear. The world itself was a tool, and patience was its weapon. Every whisper of fear, every trembling heart, every shadowed corner—each was a potential thread to pull.

And it would wait for the perfect one.

A human who might falter. A moment of doubt. A fraction of sorrow left unchecked. That was all it needed.

The darkness shifted. The air felt thicker near empty streets and abandoned buildings, lighter in places where light persisted, as though the world itself already feared it. Caligo tested boundaries, feeling for vulnerability, noting possibilities. Mara had won today, but Caligo knew it would return.

It would escape.

It would hunt again.

And when it did, it would be smarter. Sharper. More patient. More precise.

The shadows pulsed, whispering promises that only it could hear. The echoes of past victims lingered faintly, their lessons absorbed, twisted, catalogued. Each death had been a refinement, each surrender a study in human fragility. Caligo would use them all.

It waited, silent and angry, for the perfect moment—the one Mara might never see coming.

This is not over. Not for me. Not for her. Not for anyone.

Chapter Twenty-Eight

IMPORTANT MESSAGE !!!

Pain is real! Trauma is real! Losing loved ones, losing yourself. Pain comes in all shapes and forms. We all deal with it differently.

But the most important thing is.

You matter. Even if your mind is telling you otherwise right now, **you matter**—and the pain you're carrying does not define your worth.

If you are struggling with thoughts of suicide, it doesn't mean you are weak, broken, or beyond help. It means you are human and you are hurting. Pain has a way of lying to us. It tells us we are a burden. It tells us nothing will change. It tells us people would be better off without us. **Those thoughts are symptoms, not truths.**

You are worthy of help **exactly as you are**, not after you "get better," not after you explain yourself perfectly, not after you stop hurting. Right now is enough.

There are people—real people—who want to help you survive this moment. You do not have to battle your demons alone. You don't have to be strong all the time. Sometimes the bravest thing you can do is stay, breathe, and reach out.

If you're in the United States, you can call or text **988 Suicide & Crisis Lifeline** at **988**—24 hours a day, 7 days a week. You don't need the "right words." You can cry. You can be silent. You can just say, *"I'm not okay."* They will meet you where you are.

If you're outside the U.S., local crisis lines exist around the world, and emergency services are there to help keep you safe. If calling feels too hard, texting or chatting online is also an option in many places.

Please remember this: **feelings are temporary, even when they feel endless**. This chapter of your life is not the final sentence. The world would be different without you in ways you cannot see right now. Someone has been changed by your presence—maybe quietly, maybe without you ever knowing.

You are allowed to rest.

You are allowed to ask for help.

You are allowed to take up space.

You are allowed to stay.

If you can, reach out to one person today—a friend, a family member, a therapist, a hotline worker. Let someone know you're struggling. Let someone help hold the weight with you.

You are loved more than your pain will ever admit.

And you are still here for a reason—even if you can't see it yet.

If you are in immediate danger, please call your local emergency number right now.

You deserve help. You deserve care. **You deserve to live.**